LISTEN TO THE DARK

Fourteen-year-old Mark Robson is a loner. An intelligent boy, he finds it difficult to make friends, and at home his mother's attention is suffocating. He's also bullied at school and it is in the park at night, after an unpleasant encounter with some school toughs, that Mark has a strange experience which will give him a new perspective on life, a change that has implications for everyone around him.

LISTEN TO THE DARK

Maeve Henry

CHIVERS PRESS
BATH

First published 1993
by
William Heinemann Limited
an imprint of
Reed Consumer Books Limited
This Large Print edition published by
Chivers Press
by arrangement with
Reed Consumer Books Limited
1996

ISBN 0 7451 3148 4

British Library Cataloguing in Publication Data

Henry, Maeve
  Listen to the Dark.—New ed.—(Galaxy)
  Large Print Children's Books)
  I. Title   II. Series
  823.914 [J]

  ISBN 0–7451–3148–4

'Tis the year's midnight, and it is the
    day's,
Lucy's, who scarce seven hours herself
    unmasks...

... I am by her death (which word wrongs
    her)
Of the first nothing the elixir grown;
Were I a man, that I were one,
I needs must know; I should prefer,
If I were any beast,
Some ends, some means; yea plants, yea
    stones detest
And love; all, all some properties invest;
If I an ordinary nothing were,
As shadow, a light and body must be
    here.

But I am None; nor will my sun renew.
You lovers, for whose sake the lesser sun
At this time to the Goat is run
To fetch new lust and give it you,
Enjoy your summer all;
Since she enjoys her long night's festival,
Let me prepare towards her, and let me
    call
This hour her vigil, and her eve, since this
Both the year's and the day's deep
    midnight is.

From 'A Nocturnal upon St Lucy's Day'
                            John Donne

LISTEN TO THE DARK

CHAPTER ONE

Mark Robson walked round the bowling green in the weak winter sunshine and entered the garden behind it. No one was in sight. The garden was small, hidden from the rest of the park by a circle of hedges. It consisted of a square of grass, a gravel path and a long bed of shrubs and plants in front of which, at intervals, were some low wooden posts. Mark dropped his school bag on the path and went over to one of them. Shutting his eyes, he leant forward and felt the cold metal plate screwed into the top. The park around him was black, lost; his body swayed slightly and his feet shifted, seeking a stronger contact with the gravel. The pattern of raised dots under his fingers grazed his nerve endings and set up a tingling like the ghost of interpretation.

'Lavender,' he said authoritatively.

He opened his eyes quickly to check, took in the English and Latin names and the large grey green bush beyond,

1

scentless in the December afternoon. He hadn't exactly cheated, but it was impossible not to get a glimpse, as his eyes closed, of the small neat capitals beneath the Braille. He continued to stroke the dots with an absent finger as his eyes slid to the playground on the other side of the trees. Normally he went straight home from school, but today he didn't want to. His mother would see at once that something was wrong and get it out of him and then she'd be—well, the way she was about things. Uncomfortably he dropped his hand and moved to the next post.

'Rosemary.'

It was a kid's game really, not very satisfactory. He had moved on to the third post when he heard a shout and the sound of running footsteps from the direction of the trees.

'It's Porker!'

'Hallo, Porker.'

When they slowed into a walk he forced himself to turn round. His heart was pounding sickeningly. It was one thing to follow them in, another to have to face them. He wanted to pretend he

2

hadn't done it, that it was an accident. But Tim was there with them, hanging back a little, looking, Mark admitted, pretty uncomfortable; still, Tim was with them, Craig Moran's ally now, so Mark lifted his chin.

'You're not allowed to call me that. Mr Moynihan said,' he replied primly.

Craig Moran's bleached blond hair gleamed incongruously above his sallow pimpled face. He made a pantomime of carefully looking round. 'I don't seem to see Mr Moynihan, do you, Graham?'

Graham Sharkey sniggered. 'No, Craig.'

Craig stepped forward quickly and twisted Mark's arm up behind his back. The spurt of hot pain made Mark gasp and cry out. Satisfied, Craig released him with a contemptuous shove. 'We'll call you what we like, you wanker.'

Clutching his shoulder, Mark couldn't help letting his eyes slide reproachfully towards Tim. But Tim only frowned. 'He followed us in,' he said disgustedly. 'Just 'cos I'm with you.' He raised his voice. 'Why don't you give it a rest, Mark? I told you this dinner time, I'm sick of

3

going round with you.'

Craig grinned, showing his small yellow teeth. 'If he's bothering you, Tim—'

'Leave it, Craig. It's not worth it.'

But Craig didn't want to leave it. He pinioned Mark's arms and shoved him towards Graham, who heaved him back. As Mark staggered forward, Craig tripped him so that he fell heavily onto his knees. He got up, panting. Tim, he noticed with something like triumph, was shuffling his feet in the gravel and looking away towards the gate.

'Honestly, Craig,' he repeated. 'It isn't worth it.'

Craig scowled at him. 'Piss off home then, if he's such a big mate of yours.'

Tim looked at Mark. His small face showed anger and embarrassment. 'It's your own sodding fault,' he said. '*Porker*.'

He turned and began to walk away. All three of them watched him retreat, a small sandy-haired figure swamped by his new parka. Mark felt drearily puzzled. He didn't really know why he had followed them into the park, whether to shame Tim or to impress him, but this certainly wasn't what he had meant to happen. For a while nobody said anything. Then Graham came up casually and pulled Mark's head back by the hair.

'So what were you doing, Porker, when we caught you? Practising for when you go blind?'

'Know what causes that, don't you?' Craig said.

The blow came almost before he had finished speaking, banging into Mark's face, taking him by surprise. He sucked in his breath and felt, underneath the pain and much worse, the shock that would have him in tears in a minute, sooner—

'Oh, look,' Craig said sarcastically. 'Baby's crying.'

Graham drove a boot into his ankle. 'Stand up straight while we hit you,' he said. 'Haven't you got any consideration?'

But they weren't really trying, that was the humiliating thing. It was too cold and too close to tea time for them to make much of an effort. After a few more minutes of it, they left him on his knees with his face shoved in the soil, and his bag flung somewhere into the bushes.

*   *   *

When he was sure they had gone, Mark got to his feet. He felt sick and dizzy, his chest hurt and his cheek throbbed like mad. Slowly he scraped the mud off his trousers and felt in his pocket for a tissue to wipe his face. 'What's Mum going to say?' he grieved aloud. That really did it; he had to struggle hard not to start crying again. 'And wait till she hears about Tim.'

But he didn't want to tell her about Tim, not at all. It was terrible to think he would no longer be able to say, as he so enjoyed saying, 'Tim and I are going round to the model shop on Saturday morning, all right, Mum?' or 'I'm just going round to Tim's. I might not be back for tea.' And she would be even more upset than he was. She talked about Tim a lot. She was always asking after him. 'Mark has a friend now—such a nice boy,' she often said. 'They've been such good friends now for over a year.'

But Tim wasn't a nice boy, not by Mum's standards. Mark had never dared to report the words he used, even those his sisters used, at tea time in their big untidy kitchen, swearing at each other to pass the ketchup or the margarine. He rarely felt comfortable downstairs in Tim's house. The dogs made everything dirty and Tim's sisters fought, and nothing was nice. Tim's mother was hardly ever there. Tim himself often seemed a bit lost. He was the youngest child, and the only boy, and his sisters bullied him. When he was younger, in primary school, the likes of Craig and Graham had found it easy to work him up into a powerless frenzy of tears and screaming. Now he was less highly strung, he was mostly ignored by the others at school. That was one reason why Mark found Craig's sudden interest in him so hard to bear. Tim just wasn't very interesting. He had little to offer in terms of company and conversation, unless you happened to share his interest in model aircraft. Up in Tim's room after tea, Mark would flick, yawning, through Tim's old *Superman* comics, while Tim would lovingly clean his jet fighters.

'See this one, Mark? It's a Tornado, like they used in the Gulf.'

On their trips into town they often ended up bickering on a crowded pavement outside the shops.

'I thought we were going to the library.'

'You said you didn't want to go.'

'No, I didn't. I just said it was boring.'

'Well, what do you want to do that's so exciting?'

'I never said I wanted to do something else, I just said—'

'Well, why don't you go home then, if you're so fed up?'

But usually Tim stayed, and so did Mark. Being together was irritating, but being alone was worse. They only really quarrelled when Tim scented the opportunity of company elsewhere. Always up to now he had drifted back as the others grew bored with his jokes and his aeroplane talk and his endless boasting about his dad who worked on a Scottish oil rig—at least according to

8

Tim, he did. This time, though, Mark was afraid it might be different. There had been more than ritual scorn in Tim's attitude this afternoon. He had spoken angrily, hurtfully, as if from a sense of real grievance. Mark was afraid he might have lost Tim for good.

*   *   *

He searched for his bag in the bushes, and when he had found it, he stood for a little, tucking in his shirt and trying to recover his dignity. Never fight back, his mum said. It brings you down to their level. But he always had the feeling that part of her would have preferred him to fight.

Dusk was falling. In a minute the keeper would come round on his bike to lock the gates. Mark moved slowly round the garden, still unwilling to go home. It would be horrible to be blind, he thought. That was what this garden was for, blind people, and why the plants were things like lavender that you could smell. A woman called Mrs Lock had made it as a memorial to her husband, according to the plaque at the entrance. Mark shut his eyes and tried to imagine what it must be like, but he couldn't think of a thing without the shape of it coming into his mind. Did the blind see inside their heads, or did they just have darkness, hard or soft darkness, noisy or sweet?

From a distance came the faint ping of a bicycle bell. The keeper was coming to shut the gates. Mark did not want to go home. Unaccountably, he rebelled. He plunged off the path in among the trees, and stood in the protective darkness, peering out. The keeper glided up on his bike. Mark watched him drag the gate shut and draw the chain through the wrought iron bars with a heavy rattle. I'll have to climb over, he thought in disbelief. Then he realised there must still be a gate open somewhere. The park keeper would hardly lock himself in for the night. I'll step out now and walk down with him, he thought. But instead he watched the park keeper re-mount his bike and ride off, without making a move. I'm alone in the park, Mark thought with a great leap of the heart. I have it all to myself.

He sat on the swing, easing himself backwards and forwards with the slightest pressure of one foot on the ground. It was cold now, and very dark; only the fringe of street lighting beyond the bushes cast a glimmer over the playground. The shapes of the seesaw and giant slide, roundabout and horse were converted by the dark into strange and menacing things. Behind the trees at his back was the bulk of the park, the lake and the tennis courts, and the forbidden lavatories. He could hear noises, paper rattling along paths, metal creaking, the cries of sleepy birds. Mark pushed off more firmly and hauled at the cold chains of the swing. The wind blew in his face and his fingers stung, but the weight was lifting off him as he got higher and higher; twice in each arc he hung almost weightless before the fall. He was free, he was flying: he looked down over the railings at the lighted kitchen windows beyond the park. A million families were having tea and watching telly, while he was in the dark outside, and no one, not Tim, not Craig, not his mum, knew where he was.

It was too much suddenly. He jumped down from the swing when it was at its highest point, staggered and fell forward, banging his chin on the concrete. He got up, feeling humiliated. Time to go home, his cowardly conscience said, but part of him still held out. I'll go and see the lake first, he decided. The lake, and then I'll climb out.

He picked up his bag and took the path through the rocks under the trees. When he reached the boathouse on the edge of the lake, Mark decided to walk down on to the concrete apron to look at the boats. They were drawn up in a row, one long chain running through the rings in their prows secured to a metal post bedded in the concrete. Mark felt for the chain and tugged it, and the boats responded, shifting together in the water like a herd. He had never been in a boat. He had never even known there was a lake in the park until he was old enough to come by himself; his mother, for some reason, had never gone near it. Gingerly now he lowered one foot into a boat and put his weight on it. The boat slid from the bank. Feeling his leg pull away, Mark became panicky and lurched after it. For one moment he was agonisingly scissored; then he managed somehow to get his other leg off the bank and he was in. The boat rocked alarmingly and he crouched down to grasp its sides. He could feel the water lapping near his hands, the warmth of his thighs pressed together under his heavy coat and the ooze at the bottom of the boat slowly leaking into his shoes. For a moment he let himself pretend that he was out in the middle of the lake, managing his boat, water gleaming over the oars as he rowed smoothly past the dark bulk of the shore. But the boat gave another lurch as he shifted his weight and he decided rather quickly that he wanted to get out. He turned and scrambled out onto the bank, but in his hurry one of his feet slipped and the water slopped into his shoe. When he stood up on the concrete, his sock squelched unpleasantly, slimy and cold against his foot. He walked on, wincing a little at every step.

He was ready to go home now. The

strangeness of the park had begun to oppress him. He did not like the silence and the deep black shadows. He was used to town darkness, the orange glare of street lights and the blaze of car headlights. Here the darkness was profound, the close mass of trees absorbing even the light of the distant moon. Mark walked on towards the nearest gate, keeping the lake on his right. There was no sound now except the slap of water against the mud and the noise of his own hurrying footsteps. A thin thread of unease unwound in the pit of his stomach. It was getting late. He broke into a trot, trying not to panic, pressing forward towards the gap in the trees where the path led off at right angles to the gate. But before he reached it he shied suddenly like an animal and ran, his head averted, from the lake. He struggled through the bushes and when he hit a path he dropped his bag and stood, hands on his knees, fighting to get his breath. The lake was behind him, and as his level of fear dropped, he was able to recall what had happened. He had run into a little patch of darkness, scarcely discernible from the shadows of the trees, but absolutely different. Even now he felt the chill of it. As he straightened up there was a sound from the same place. It was faint, it hardly reached his ears, but he recognised it. Something was calling his name.

CHAPTER TWO

The sitting room was small, and with the heating turned up high, almost unbearably hot. Mark sat eating his tea in silence, wedged into the corner of the settee with a tray on his knees and the coffee table menacing his shins. His mother sat in an armchair across the room, knitting aggressively, fast precise fingers clicking away to produce the purple mohair sweater she was making for a friend. She was a small upright woman with short grey hair and glasses, neatly dressed in cream shirt and dark green cords.

'You can take that plate into the kitchen yourself,' she said, tugging at the ball of wool. 'I'm not going to wait on you, coming in at all hours.'

'Sorry, Mum.'

'If you'd been out any longer, I'd have got on to the police.'

'I said I'm sorry.'

'I heard you. Pity you weren't sorry two hours ago when your tea started to spoil.'

'Tastes all right to me.'

She looked at him sharply. 'I don't think you realise . . .' she began severely, but her attention was caught by something on the television. Her next words were lost in a roar of laughter and applause from the studio audience. '. . . never mind the state of your shoes. It'll take me ages to get them clean.'

'I'll do them, then.'

'Don't be ridiculous,' she said at once. 'You've got homework.'

Mark went on hacking at his pizza, dried up and hardened by its long stay in the oven. He hated it when she was angry with him, really hated it. He hoped she had finished complaining, but when the commercials came on she started again.

'And there's all that mud on your coat.

16

I don't know how I'm going to get that off. Where did you say you were mucking about?'

'In the park,' Mark said softly. As he spoke the feeling of panic returned. Stinging bile rushed up into his throat and he shut his eyes, praying he wasn't going to be sick. When he opened them again his mother was staring at him.

'The park closes at four-thirty this time of year.'

'I know.'

'So where were you?'

'I told you, in the park.' He hesitated, then added in a low voice, 'It was them, Mum. They wouldn't let me go.'

It was probably the first direct lie he had told her, but he couldn't, he couldn't tell her the truth. He was too afraid. And as he watched her expression soften into concern, he felt guiltily comforted.

She put down her knitting and came over to him. 'You silly boy,' she said. 'Why didn't you tell me at once?'

He shrugged. 'Don't know.'

She tilted his head back and pushed the hair from his forehead. 'Did they give you this nasty knock?'

17

He nodded.

'I'll put some cream on it later,' she said. 'Don't I keep telling you to walk home with Tim or some of the girls that live round here? Those rotten pigs won't pick on you if you're with someone else.'

'I know, but . . .'

'And I'll give you another letter to take to the school.'

'Oh, Mum,' he said glumly. 'I wish you wouldn't.'

'Somebody has to stick up for you, since you won't stick up for yourself,' she said sharply. 'Somebody has to try and make those teachers do what they're paid for. No, Mark, I'm sorry, but I do know what I'm talking about. I'm very disappointed with the attitude they've taken to all this. They've simply ignored the last two letters I sent.'

He shrugged uncomfortably and turned towards the television. But that only made her raise her voice.

'This business tonight is the absolute last straw. Practically kidnapping you in the park for three hours. If that school won't do anything, I'll go directly to their parents.'

Mark fervently hoped she wouldn't. But there was no way he could get out of it, other than admitting he had lied. Instead he got up and began to edge his way round the coffee table towards the door.

'There's your pudding in the kitchen,' his mother said. 'Chocolate mousse.'

'I'll have it later,' he said. 'I'm going to do my maths.'

'You know, you could do your homework downstairs like you used to,' she suggested in a gentler voice. 'We could switch off the telly and put on the Tchaikovsky tape.'

'Tchaikovsky?' Mark made a face.

His mother was hurt as well as angry. 'There's no need to be rude. You used to like it very much.'

'Well, that was before I started listening to Shostakovitch. And anyway, I can't do maths to classical stuff. I want to listen to Motorhead on my headphones.'

Rather pointedly his mother did not reply, but got up to turn up the volume of the television.

Feeling dismissed, Mark paused in the

doorway to make some witty comment, but nothing came to him. His mother was sitting with her back to him, apparently absorbed in her programme. Mark looked across the room at his father, sitting in a corner of the small bay window with the pages of the local paper spread out across his knees. As usual he was ignoring everything that went on. He was a big man, with grey in his hair and large reddish hands. Mark watched him for a moment longer as he felt for the glass of whisky under his chair and had a sip. Then he shut the door on both his parents and went upstairs.

His bedroom was at the front of the house over the hallway, next to his parents' room. It felt chilly after the heat of the sitting room. Mark switched on the fan heater and began to lay out his homework books on the card table he used as a desk. But it was no good. Now he was alone the fear was back, out of all control. He paused, a book in his hand, and stood motionless. Then, setting the book down with extreme care, he scrambled like an animal towards his bed. From under the covers he lay staring at his posters of the mammal kingdom and the solar system. His thumb crept up towards his mouth. His eyes tracked the pattern of the wallpaper and minutely examined the cartoon stickers on the scarred brown wardrobe. The surface of things had grown very thin and underneath was darkness.

He lay like that for what seemed a long time. The core of himself was occupied by fear, his reason pushed out to the edges. He could not think about what had happened in the park, only remember his fear and his flight, the desperate scramble over the railings, tearing his shirt and almost losing a shoe. Now it was here with him, he could feel it, the thing he had run away from. His terror grew so intense that he seemed to be reduced to a single point of consciousness. There, in the centre, he was passionless, an observer. As he grasped this, the grip of fear lessened in its intensity. He threw back the covers and got shakily to his feet. He went to the window and lifted the curtain. The air was cold on his face, the glass silvered with condensation. On the other side the

21

dark was pressing in.

'What do you want?' he said aloud. Nothing happened. For a full minute he waited and then, unaccountably, the fear lifted. His room returned to normal; the surface of things resumed their depth. He ran his fingers over the green baize covering the card table, dipping into the ragged hole near the edge. He touched his books. Then he picked up his Walkman, fitted the headphones to his ears, sat down and began to work.

He got through the maths easily enough. It was quadratic equations, which he enjoyed doing, gathering the xs and the ys, multiplying, subtracting, obtaining the answer. All the time the heavy metal sound was ripping through his head and he found himself working to its adrenalin rhythm, banging down the answers like bombs. He pulled the headphones off when he picked up his history file. That called for something less mindless. He reached under the bed for a tape the music teacher at school, Mr Potter, had lent him, of four baroque trumpet concertos. He turned the volume down to medium and, with his ears receiving little shocks of felicity, began to flip through his notes. His class were working on a special project this term, tracing the history of the town from its mention in the Domesday Book to the present. Nothing much seemed to have happened until the Industrial Revolution, when iron ore was discovered in the hills nearby and the steel mills, all closed now, had transformed a fishing village into a raw boom town.

Some of the class had gone round visiting old people, taping their recollections of the War. To Mark's embarrassment, when the tapes were played in class, he had recognised the voice of his own grandmother, complaining from her chair in the council home lounge about the breakdown of family life: '*I never thought I'd end my days in one of these places. I was brought up to look after my own and I expected my own to look after me. I suppose that sounds naive to you, but we weren't so materialistic as people are now. They don't want to be bothered with you unless you can offer something in return. In my day we had nothing, but what we had, we shared.'*

Mark, who still resented her greedy monopolising of the Quality Street at Christmas, frankly doubted it. And he felt very angry at the implication that her family had abandoned her in the home. Mum went round every Wednesday to change her library books and buy her Beecham's pills. And he went too, sometimes, when Mum insisted.

Just then he heard something outside the door. As he pushed back his headphones his mother came into the room without knocking, and set down a cup of tea on the table.

'It's gone nine o'clock, did you realise?' she said brightly.

'Mmm.'

He turned over a page without looking up. She put her hand on the back of his chair and leant forward to see what he was reading. The familiar, rather stifling sweetness of her scent and talc engulfed him.

'You know, you'd be much more comfortable downstairs,' she said. 'What's that, geography?'

'History. I've hardly started.'

'Not for tomorrow, though, I bet. Why don't you come downstairs and watch a bit of telly with us?' She touched his file dismissively. 'They can't want you to do that much.'

'In a minute, Mum.'

'It's always in a minute with you.' Her voice sharpened resentfully. 'You've been up here on your own for gone an hour and a half.'

Mark turned his head reluctantly. She was so close he could not get her whole face into focus, only the chalky grain of the skin on the side of her nose, and the sad lines dragging at her mouth.

'But I've got a lot to do,' he said angrily. 'I haven't practised my trumpet yet.'

'Well, that's one thing you can cross off your list for definite,' she retorted. 'It's far too late. The little girls next door go to bed at eight, you know that.'

Mark sat alone for another five minutes, trying to read, then followed her downstairs.

*   *   *

They were watching the news. His father had moved, with his glass and bottle, to the settee. When Mark sat down next to him he turned and stared, his eyes thick with drink and sentiment. Mark looked away quickly. He didn't know how his mother could stand it. But she was happy now he was downstairs. She made loud comments on the news while he wrote up his history notes.

'Watch his eyes, Mark, while he's saying that. You can see he doesn't believe a word of it ... Oh, just look at that dress! We could go on holiday for half of what she spent on that.'

At ten o'clock he had his chocolate mousse, and at half-past ten he went up to bed. Normally he read for a little while, Asimov or Jeffrey Archer, but tonight he got out his trumpet mouthpiece and lay in the dark buzzing tunes until he heard his parents coming upstairs together and turned over guiltily and went to sleep.

CHAPTER THREE

The following afternoon, Mark stood in the goal mouth while the players fought it out deep in the opposite half. It had been a pig of a day. Under his shuffling feet the mud was stiff with frost. His breath smoked and he had tucked his fists into his armpits for warmth. Behind the houses the sun was going down, blood-red and massive like a dying world. The voices of the two defenders gossiping near him floated, like the sharp yells from down the pitch, remote, free of personal concern. It was the last lesson of the afternoon. In ten or fifteen minutes he would be changing indoors. In half an hour he would be home.

Break had been the worst. He had very few lessons with Tim, only games and art and CDT, so he was used to not seeing him then. But when the bell for break rang, half-hoping, he made his way to their usual place, an alcove opposite the vending machines in the hall. Tim wasn't there. Mark walked round the playground on his own, with his hood up against the wind and the possible comments of the boys lounging in groups near the perimeter netting. When he couldn't put off going to the toilet any longer, he ducked in and tried not to see Tim sitting on the edge of a basin, coughing as he shared a cigarette with Graham. Mark left without washing his hands, blundering out through their laughter, more upset by the cigarette than anything else. Tim had always agreed with him that smoking was stupid.

At dinner time he had gone to Mr Moynihan's office and given his mother's letter to the secretary. Mr Moynihan, fortunately, was out, so Mark was spared the usual embarrassing little chat about whether he was happy at home, and did he have a girlfriend yet. He was late joining the dinner queue but Craig saw him and worked his way steadily up to stand next to him. He looked at Mark's bruised forehead, grinned, and said nothing. Then, as Gloria Baker passed them with her tray, he shoved Mark towards her with sudden force.

'Get your leg over her, Porker! You'd flatten anyone else you tried it with.'

Gloria, a large girl in the third year, and Mark narrowly avoided collision, and each other's eyes. For some reason, whenever it happened, he blamed Gloria more than Craig. He almost hated her.

*   *   *

The memory of Craig prompted a quick check on his whereabouts. He was still far down the pitch, on the losing team, his blond hair flying in his desperate attempts to clear the ball to his waiting strikers. Behind him, yelling encouragement and avoiding the ball, was Tim. Mark looked away at once. On the next pitch the girls were playing hockey. Gloria Baker stood in the goal nearest to Mark, wearing huge shoes and shin pads, waving her hockey stick about and dropping it. The defenders, thin girls in glasses, stood together chatting, while in the middle of the pitch the play was fierce. Mark watched the legs moving under regulation skirts, mottled or brown or creamy. Graham claimed he had touched up a girl in the cinema, and Craig carried a pack of condoms round with him, sliding them unwrapped into the exercise books of girls in class. Mark grew hot and heavy thinking about that, thinking about parts of girls, running and re-running the film in his head until the shrill bubbling of the hockey teacher's whistle brought his thoughts to a guilty stop. The girls pulled up obediently and began to leave the pitch. Twitching his underpants surreptitiously, Mark turned towards the road where he saw a middle-aged man in a fawn mac standing at the fence watching the girls.

'Dirty old man,' he said automatically, then froze. It was his father. Dimly he was aware of the noise behind him, of someone screaming near his ear; then the ball struck him on the back of the knees and he stumbled forward over the line.

'Porker, you lardarse!'

'They've equalised, you stupid git!'

As he got to his feet, Mr Rudham blew the final whistle. Craig ran up at once and patted Mark on the cheek.

'Thanks, pal. You're a great goalie—to play against.'

Mark hardly noticed him. He stared across the field at his father who, as the girls dispersed, turned and began to walk in the direction of town.

He wasn't a dirty old man. He couldn't be. He was Dad. Then Mark's own hot thoughts returned into his mind, horrible and familiar, and he felt deeply ashamed, as if he and his father had been caught together, exposing themselves. When he got to the changing room he sat down on the wooden bench and slowly pulled off his football boots and his socks. The tiles were cold and slippery with trampled mud and water from the shower, and it was unpleasant to have to put his feet on them. He sat in a hollow roar of voices, ignoring the jeers of the boys next to him, still on about the goal he had let in, and beyond that the hoarse bark of Mr Rudham, chivvying them all into the shower. His dad hadn't seen him, that was the main thing, and as far as he knew no one else had recognised him at the fence. Best just to bury it,

31

pretend it hadn't happened. He got up, finished undressing, and padded across to the shower with his towel clutched to his stomach.

'Pathetic, Robson,' bawled Mr Rudham as he passed. 'Absolutely pathetic. What are you?'

'Pathetic, sir.'

'And I want to see you *wet* when you come out of there, understand?'

'Sir.'

Craig was in a good mood after the equaliser.

'Hello, Marko!' he yelled through the steam. 'Watch out lads, there won't be much room in here now the Elephant Man's arrived.'

Mark dipped his arms and legs in the hot spray and ducked out again, slipping behind Mr Rudham's back to regain the bench. As he got dressed he looked round furtively for Tim. He was standing across the room, struggling to balance while pulling on a sock. In Craig's absence no one was talking to him. Among the group of laughing and joking boys he was, like Mark, alone, and because of it Mark felt a faint

32

stirring of hope. Craig would get bored with him. Tim would come back.

In the meantime, he finished dressing and left alone. He walked slowly, thinking about his father. He had never really thought about him before, just endured him, like school or bad weather. But now he was faced with it. He couldn't believe his father was guilty of anything wrong. After all, he didn't do anything, just sat at home drinking whisky when Mum was there and walked round town by himself when she was at work. Anyone could stop walking round to watch a hockey match. But then it struck him, with a rekindling of his shame and fear, that other people's fathers didn't. Other people's fathers had jobs and hobbies, decorated the spare room and went on holiday. Other people's fathers *talked*. He struggled to remember what his father had been like before his redundancy notice two years ago, if he had been any different. Nothing came to mind. It was Mum who had brought him up. When he tried to picture his father he saw only her. He could remember millions of things she had done. She had played the records he listened to when he was small, *Peter and the Wolf* and *The World of Ballet*—he could still remember waving his legs around to the tunes to make her laugh. She had taken him to his first concert at the town hall when he was eight. And when he had been given his trumpet at school it was Mum he had needed, rushing up to the supermarket where she worked and queuing up with the real customers to show her it. They had been extraordinarily close, wrapped up in each other. Dad had always been outside the picture, uninvolved, alone.

So Dad hadn't changed. Whatever he was, he was the same. If anything had changed in the family, Mark thought guiltily, it was between himself and Mum, and that was his fault. He somehow couldn't get on with her any more. When he was little he had believed everything she told him, but now it embarrassed him to hear her talking, saying things he knew to be silly. Last week they had had an argument because she insisted that Dracula came from the Transvaal. He hated going to the library with her because she chose popular romances, and then made him carry them for her. It would have been all right, of course, only she hadn't noticed that he had changed. She still thought they should do everything together. She wanted him to share all his interests with her, even things she couldn't understand, like computer magazines and Go. When Tim came round she expected them both to stay downstairs and play Monopoly or something to keep her company. He fervently wished that Dad would get a job, start acting like a normal person, *wake up*, so that Mum would have someone else to think about, and he would have a bit of space to breathe.

Maybe Dad was too old to change. They were both old, older than Tim's parents, and older, somehow, than their age. Last year, after the school concert, Mr Potter the new music teacher had come up to Mum and said, 'Mrs Robson senior, I presume? How very nice that you could come and see your grandson in action.' He thought Mum's friend Win, from the supermarket, was Mrs Robson. Mum had never forgiven him.

She made acid remarks if Mark mentioned Mr Potter's opinion of anything, and he had long since given up trying to play her the tapes Mr Potter lent him. It was a pity, because Mr Potter was easily Mark's favourite teacher, and music his favourite subject: he planned to choose it as one of his options for GCSE.

'Which reminds me,' he said aloud. He had a form about that in his bag.

*　　　*　　　*

He had reached home and, as he pushed open the door, he heard voices. Win was there, Mum's friend from the supermarket, the one she was knitting the sweater for. His instinct was to bolt upstairs, but as soon as they heard him in the hall, his mother called out, 'Win's here, love,' so he had to go in and say hello.

Win was lolling on the settee, balancing an ashtray on her knee. 'Here's your brainy son,' she said in the lazy way Mark hated. 'Still top of the class in everything, are you?'

'I s'pose.'

'God, I wish mine were like that.' She turned back to Mark's mother. 'Did I tell you we got a letter from Tony's teacher saying he's been nicking off the school? Can you imagine! Brian gave him a right rollicking, but I don't know if it's done any good. You just don't know what goes on in their little minds, do you?'

She had a rasping voice from too many cigarettes and cropped blonde hair. Mark slumped into his father's chair by the window, watching the two of them together, comparing Win's purple jump suit and white cowboy boots with his mother's sensible clothes. People's mothers shouldn't look like Win, he thought, with faint protest. He never could understand why Mum was friends with her.

'Brian took me out to that new place on Market Street, what's it called? But you don't go in for dancing, do you, Jean?' Win said.

'I haven't been out dancing since before Mark was born,' his mother said with a small smile. 'When you've a family...'

Win fidgeted, rolling her cigarette on the edge of the ashtray. 'You should get out more,' she said vaguely. 'Brian wants us to book one of those skiing holidays for January. He saw a good one in the paper. Romania, or somewhere. Still, we can afford to on his money. I don't know how you put up with it, Jean, I really don't.'

His mother crossed her ankles and looked down at them with the same small smile.

'And do you still go over to your sister's every month?'

His mother looked up, her face suddenly sharp.

'Now that's something I couldn't endure.' Win blew out a long plume of smoke and shook her head. 'I couldn't go through what you went through, Jean. It would have torn me and Brian apart, and there you and Alan are—'

'Mark,' his mother said in a chilly voice. 'Fetch Win's coat for her, will you? It's in the hall.'

He could hear their voices through the door as he went out, Win's high and apologetic, his mother's recriminatory.

'I'd no idea that was the time,' Win exclaimed as Mark re-entered the room. 'Thanks for giving me a shove, Jean. I must be on my way, or Brian'll think I've run away with the milkman. Chance'd be a fine thing.' Win was on her feet, and she took the leather jacket out of Mark's arms without even looking at him. 'So long,' she said. 'See you tomorrow.'

They heard her go out, slamming the door.

'Now your tea'll be late,' his mother said. 'She says she doesn't mind me getting on, but I don't like anyone in the kitchen when I'm working.'

'What did she mean?'

'Mean? About what?'

'About going to your sister's.'

'What do you think she meant?' his mother said. 'We've hardly got the money for my bus fares into town, that's what she meant. Now stop asking stupid questions, Mark, and let me get on.'

Mark went upstairs, banging his bag up every step.

It made no better sense when he got to his room. Mum's sister lived over a hundred miles away, and it was a difficult journey, involving a change of trains and then a long bus ride at the other end. When his mother went, she came back white with exhaustion, her nerves so stretched that Mark usually went to bed early to avoid being snarled at. She went there and back on the same day, every fourth Sunday of the month. There seemed to be no reason why she should be so devoted; Auntie Eileen, Mark remembered from a Christmas visit a few years ago, was rather smart, something of a career woman. 'She's on her own now Ken's left her,' his mother said. 'She's lonely. She appreciates a visit.'

She hardly ever came to see them, though. But Mum was like that, devoted to her family to the point, it seemed to Mark, of complete unreason. Look at the way she went to visit Gran.

He took out his books and tried to work, but his mind kept drifting back to the problem of his parents, and especially of his father. Sometime later he heard the door go downstairs, which meant Dad was back. His mother called upstairs shortly afterwards to say the tea was ready, but Mark put off going down. When he did eventually enter the kitchen, she had already finished dishing up the chicken pie, mashed potatoes and peas.

'Didn't you hear me?' she said. 'I called you twice.'

'I was busy with something,' Mark said, not looking at his father.

They all three sat down, Mark and his father side by side, his mother squeezed onto the end next to Mark, her chair backing into the refrigerator. Nobody said anything for a while. There were the noises of eating and the buzz of the little radio, still on beside the cooker. The neon light made a black oblong of the window and on the windowsill his mother's spider plants trailed long, brown-edged, leaves.

'I got this pie half-price,' his mother said, breaking the silence. 'Not too bad, is it? That's the one good thing about working in a supermarket, you spot all the things about to expire.'

Mark grunted. He was surreptitiously watching his father, who ate with slow thoroughness, first his mashed potato, then his pie.

'And how was school?' his mother persisted.

'All right.'

'Nothing to tell me about it?'

'Not really,' Mark said.

His father began to scoop up his peas. Mark watched one of them fall from his fork and bounce onto the floor. Unexpectedly, his father cleared his throat and spoke.

'There was a terrible thing in the paper today. A man assaulting a girl of thirteen. Terrible. Leicester, it was.'

'Please, Alan,' said Mark's mother. 'Not while we're eating.'

'A girl of thirteen,' his father repeated. 'I couldn't stop thinking about it. I thought, at least there are some things she never—'

'*Alan!*'

His mother's tone was unmistakable. His father took another scoop of peas and shoved them into his mouth.

Mark pushed his plate away, feeling sick. His mother never spoke in that tone of urgency unless she felt personally threatened. So was that really what was the matter with his father, that he couldn't stop thinking about thirteen-year-old girls?

'Aren't you going to finish your pie, Mark?' his mother said reproachfully. 'There's yoghurt in the fridge, Alan, strawberry or fruits of the forest.'

'I don't want any,' Mark said quickly. 'And I don't want a cup of tea. I'm going back upstairs, all right? I've got a lot to do.'

And before she could get at him, he went.

Once Mark was in his room, instead of continuing with his homework, he got out his trumpet and began to play. He went through his scales, first tongued then slurred, and then began to work on a new piece in his study book. It comforted him to hold the trumpet, to feel its familiar fit against his mouth, slightly to the left of true, to feel the metal gradually take warmth from his grip. He tapped out the rhythm of a tricky bit on the table top with the flat of his hand and even tried to sing it when he had to. 'Da-da *da*, da-di-di-*da* ba, *ba*. Be easier if we had a piano.'

43

His fingers felt clumsy and sluggish, and when he tried to play the piece faster the notes all bunched and he couldn't keep proper time. He kept on, repeating the phrases until his lungs ached and he had to give up with a gasp. As he shook out the spit from the trumpet he realised he had come to a decision. He had to ask her.

*   *   *

The living room door was open, and she was sitting alone, leafing through a magazine.

'Where's Dad?'

'In the bathroom.'

Mark nodded, reluctant now the opportunity had been given. His eyes were caught by the bright and busy television screen, and for a few seconds he let himself watch it, purpose suspended. Then, trying not to be scared, he said, 'Mum, something did happen at school today. I saw Dad watching from the road when I was playing football.'

'Good.' She smiled at him. 'I hope your side was winning.'

44

'He wasn't watching me.' He brought himself to say it. 'He was watching the girls, Mum.'

He saw at once from her face that she knew. She let the magazine fall and went on looking at her hands instead. He felt himself starting to panic, found himself continuing to talk, trying to take it back, to deny it for both of them. 'I know it sounds—well, it is stupid, isn't it? Anyone can stop and watch a hockey match—so why not him? But, you know, Mum, he is so funny, and there's all this stuff in the papers like he was on about just now, and though it's really stupid, I couldn't help wondering...'

And suddenly she relaxed. She looked across at him with a smile of pure amusement. She was having a hard time not to laugh. 'You were wondering whether your father was a *pervert*?'

'Yes,' said Mark. 'Yes.'

'Oh, *Mark*,' she said. 'Honestly!'

He didn't know whether he felt more relieved or foolish. 'I don't know why you think it's so funny,' he said rather crossly. 'Look at him, Mum. He's *weird*. Even Tim asked about it, the first time he

45

came to the house. And you were worried when I told you. I could see it in your face, so don't pretend you weren't.'

It sounded very weak and silly now, even to his own ears; he wanted her to stop looking at him with that special expression of superior adult wisdom and kindness.

'Mark,' she said, and smiled, and held out her hand. 'Marky, come here.'

Reluctantly, he crossed the room to her and stood beside her chair.

'Can you be very grown-up if I tell you something?' she said.

'All right,' he answered suspiciously.

It was a long moment before she said anything. Then, 'Have you ever wondered why we only had you?' she asked.

'No,' he said, surprised. It had never occurred to him that they might have wanted more, and he couldn't see any connection with what had gone before. 'I thought you were happy with just me,' he said, a little offended.

'I am, and I always have been,' she said. 'But your father—well, when the doctor said it wasn't safe to have any

46

more, and I'd had such a bad time with you, so it was obviously for the best—your father really took it badly. He so much wanted a girl, you see, Mark. These things are irrational, so there's no way we can blame him, though I do think he might have taken a bit more interest in you when you were small. Then, after he lost his job and everything, he just seemed to retreat more and more into his own world. Sometimes he even talks as if he *had* a daughter. But you needn't worry, it's quite safe. It's not that sort of interest in little girls at all.'

'Oh,' said Mark, 'I see.' But he didn't. He was quite lost.

His mother was looking at him anxiously. 'I shouldn't have told you,' she said. 'Only I couldn't have you thinking something worse about him, could I?'

Mark nodded vaguely. 'I think he should see a whatsit, a psychiatrist.' Then it really struck him. He said angrily, 'You mean he blames me because I'm not a girl? He's not interested in me because I'm a boy?'

'I told you you'd have to be very

47

grown-up about it,' his mother said. 'And I've always tried very hard to make it up to you.' She smiled at him and there were tears standing in her eyes. 'You've always been *my* best boy.'

Mark tried to smile back, but he couldn't. As soon as she would let him, he moved away. Inside he was boiling with resentment, towards *him*, of course, but also towards her. It was wrong, it made him feel horrible, but he blamed her for telling him. And there was more than that: he hated being her best boy. It felt—it felt like drowning. She must have seen how he felt because her expression changed suddenly. She looked injured, outraged, almost as if he had thrown her love back in her face. She sat forward angrily, and was about to speak when the door opened. Mark's father came into the room. He grunted at both of them, sat down and picked up his newspaper. The silence was uncomfortable, and Mark started to blether.

'Oh, and that was the other thing I came down for, Mum. I need you to sign my form for my options. I was so pleased; Mr Potter stopped me today and asked me if I was willing to do music. I've got the form upstairs.'

He only meant it as something to cover his retreat to the door, something that would get him safely out of the room. Her reaction took him completely by surprise. Her face puckered as if she had bitten on a lemon.

'Then you'll have to tell him you've got better things to do, won't you?'

Mark looked at her uncertainly. 'You're joking, Mum, aren't you? You know I'm going to do music.'

She wouldn't meet his eyes. She looked away and picked up her magazine.

'But you can't mean that,' Mark said. 'You always liked me being interested in music. You bought me records. You listened to my exam pieces on the trumpet. I thought it was something you wanted me to do.'

'It's a very nice hobby for you,' she said, turning the pages of the magazine. 'Very nice, but I wouldn't take it any more seriously than that.'

Mark couldn't believe what he was

49

hearing. He looked round at his father with a faint residual hope, but there was no sign he was even listening. 'Please don't joke about it, Mum,' he said, growing pinker. 'I'm sorry if I upset you just now, but this is something really important.'

She looked up, meeting his eyes. 'I'm not in the least upset,' she said. 'But I really can't sign any piece of paper allowing you to waste your time at school. You need to do something useful, something an employer will appreciate. You need maths and physics, and languages, things like that.'

'But I can do those as well,' Mark said, struggling to stay calm. 'I've got eight options, Mum, you don't seem to realise. I don't *need* biology, or German. And Mr Potter says if I miss out on the GCSE, I can't do A-level.'

'A-level? So now we're getting to the truth,' she said. It was her turn to appeal across the room. 'Hear that, Alan? That teacher's put it into his head to do music A-level.' She turned back to Mark. 'Who do you think you are, Yehudi Menuhin?'

'I couldn't be,' Mark retorted, stung.

'He plays the violin, not the trumpet.'

Her face darkened. 'Don't be cheeky,' she snapped.

He made one last effort. 'Mr Potter says—'

'Oh, I'm sick of that man's name!' she exclaimed. 'Ever since he came to the school it's been Mr Potter this, and Mr Potter that.'

'But he thinks I'm good, Mum,' Mark protested, getting dangerously close to tears. 'He says I should think about getting private lessons, even my own trumpet.'

'Does he really?' she said grimly. 'Well, I'd like to hear him say it to *me*, with what I have to keep you on. When did he say all this?'

'Lunch time. We had band practice.'

'Well, you tell him you've decided to keep your music for lunch times,' she said. 'Tell him you've decided to do biology.'

Mark turned brick red. His hands fiddled in his pockets. He was so angry he couldn't keep still. He was afraid of his anger, afraid of what it might make him say or do. Suddenly it rushed out of

51

him in terrible bitter words. 'I hate you,' he told her. 'You're just jealous. You're jealous because I'm better than you and because it's Mr Potter that's helping me. I *am* good at music, Mum, but you won't admit it. You're a ... a bloody Philistine, that's what. And you're a mean cow, as well. I bet even Tim's mum would help him if he wanted to do something as badly as I want this. But you won't help me.'

Breathless, he stopped, feeling exhilarated now as well as afraid. He had never spoken to his mother like that in the whole of his life. But the exhilaration vanished when he saw the expression on her face. She moved towards him and he moved towards the door.

'How dare you?' she said in an awful voice. 'How dare you throw Tim's mother in my face! Haven't I always done my best for you? Tim would never dare to speak to his mother the way you just spoke to me.'

'Wouldn't he?' Mark retorted. 'Shows how much you know.'

He ran out of the room and up the stairs to his own room where he threw himself down on his bed, scared that she was coming after him. He was shocked at himself and at her; what was he doing with such feelings of angry malice? He felt like crying, and after a while he did, lifting his head from the pillow between sobs to listen for comfort from downstairs. He heard nothing. She wasn't coming up. His unease deepened and he stopped crying. Had he said something unforgiveable? It wasn't right to say you hated someone. It was a terrible thing to say to Mum, and anyway it wasn't true. But if she had meant what she said, if she really meant it . . .

'She's got no *right*,' he said, and rolled off the bed onto his feet. He slouched over to his desk and tried to look over his French for tomorrow. But everything was going wrong. Mr Potter was the only teacher that really liked him. None of the others did, not really. It was funny, because they were supposed to like the clever ones and he was clever, top, in fact, in nearly everything. Yet when he put up his hand in, say, history, Miss Rogers ignored it, and if he spoke without putting up his hand, she said, 'Thank you, Mark,' in a funny dry way that made him feel terrible. But when Mr Potter asked a question he always winked at Mark as if to say, 'This isn't for you, let the others have a go; I know *you* know.' He never felt he had to show off in Mr Potter's lessons. But he couldn't explain to Mum that it wasn't just music that mattered, but Mr Potter. She thought everything was fine with all the teachers because they gave him good marks for his exams, and she certainly didn't want to hear how much he needed Mr Potter. She wanted to hear that all he really needed was her.

Meanwhile, she was sitting downstairs, angry with him. The longer Mark stayed in his room, the more he felt the pressure of it. In the end he went down, without any clear idea of what to say, just hoping that somehow if he found the right words, if he said he was sorry well enough, everything would work out.

CHAPTER FOUR

When he reached the hall, he hesitated. He couldn't make himself go into the living room straight away. Instead he went up to the mirror framed with a gilt sunburst and looked at himself against the biscuit coloured walls and the orange carpet, and the humped coats. Vaguely comforted, he pushed open the living room door, but only his father was there.

'Where's Mum?'

His father didn't look up from his paper. 'Upstairs.'

'D'you mean in the spare room? I didn't hear her go.'

That was where she went when she was upset. Mark swung the door backwards and forwards, feeling terrible. His father coughed and scratched his chest through the thick dark wool of his pullover. Mark said, 'Should I make her some tea or something?' His father only grunted. Mark wanted to snatch away his newspaper and rip it up. 'Don't you care that she's upset?' he asked nastily.

His father looked up, irritated. 'You're the one that upset her, not me.'

Mark banged out of the room and went into the kitchen to make the tea.

When it was ready he took it upstairs. She was sitting in the dark. He knocked and she answered faintly and the light came on under the door. He went in. She was sitting on the end of the bed, her fingers digging into the flowered quilt. One sheepskin slipper had fallen off and her narrow foot, in a pink cotton sock, looked small and vulnerable. Her face had a shiny, sulky look and her eyes were red with crying. She took the offered tea without looking at him. Mark had the feeling for an odd moment that she was the child and he the adult comforter. He said, 'I'm sorry, Mum. I didn't mean to upset you.'

'Upset!' Her voice was thick with tears. She clutched the mug of tea, but didn't drink from it.

'I didn't mean any of that,' Mark continued. 'About—about hating you, or anything.'

She did not respond. He knew more

was needed and he searched his mind tiredly for something else to say, something that had worked in the past. 'Did you have a bad day?'

'It was fine until you started. First you say things about your father, then you say things about me. I've been sitting up here wondering where we went wrong.'

'Oh, Mum.' He couldn't stand it. 'I've already told you I didn't mean what I said.'

'I know what you meant,' she said. 'I heard you. I'm the Philistine. I'm the one who doesn't understand your precious artistic soul. Of course not. I'm only the one that does the washing and the cooking, and sees there's a meal on the table when you come in. That's all you want from me, either of you. I'm only a domestic servant in this house. My needs and my opinions don't count for anything.'

'Of course they do,' Mark said soothingly. He knew where he was now; this was a familiar routine.

'No, they don't. So long as you get your dinner and your pocket money you don't even notice how I'm feeling.

When's the last time you spent any time with your father and me without having to be asked? You'd rather moon about upstairs on your own, or go out with Tim.'

Mark opened his mouth and shut it again. Now, while she was raging, was not the best moment to tell her about Tim.

'And when I hear you go on about Mr Potter as if he was the only person in the world who'd ever done anything for you, it makes me feel so hurt.'

The truth in it made Mark wince. 'I don't go on about him that much,' he said. 'Do I?'

'You should hear yourself,' his mother retorted. 'You'd think he was the only teacher in that school. You'd think he'd invented music, when it's *me* that started you off, *me* that helped you all this time.'

Mark bit back the obvious question. 'I know that, Mum,' he said.

'And don't you think I'd know if you needed your own trumpet and private lessons?' she continued. 'Don't you think I want you to be as good as you possibly can?'

Mark looked away, afraid to speak. He didn't know, he really didn't.

'Don't you think your mum knows you better than Mr Potter?' she said very gently.

He didn't know, he didn't know, and he was afraid to say. The pressure of her gentleness was drowning him. 'It's OK,' he gasped. 'It's all right, Mum. I'll tell him tomorrow. I'll do biology.'

She smiled a sad little smile. 'It really is for the best,' she said. 'I only want to do what's right for you, Marky.'

Mark couldn't look at her. He got up, afraid to stay and afraid to leave, trying desperately not to think about what he had just agreed to. He made an effort to look around the room. It was decorated quite prettily in pink and white, with curtains that matched the quilt and the cushions in the wicker chair. It was the only room in the house on which some thought and care could be seen to have been expended. It should, he thought angrily, belong to a different house, to happier people.

'Sit down, Mark,' said his mother behind him. She sounded cheerful, almost recovered now. 'Tell me about school today.'

He looked round, and she patted the bed beside her. Mechanically he went over and sat down; he couldn't do otherwise. She put her arm round him and he wanted to tell her not to, but instead he let it lie heavily across his shoulders.

'Tell me about school,' she said again. 'Something interesting must have happened.'

So he told her about the French test and about Craig in the dinner queue, all of it meaningless. She smiled and frowned and made sympathetic noises. He felt numb, too defeated even to be resentful. And why should he blame her anyway? He was the one who had given in.

He couldn't manage to sit next to her for very long. He got up and went to the window. Misinterpreting his movements, his mother smiled.

'Homework,' she said. 'Always homework. Poor Mark. Still, those sciences are what a boy should be doing, aren't they? I do worry about you sometimes, being brought up by your poor mum practically on her own. A lot of musicians aren't exactly, you know, the sort of company a young boy should have, especially if he's a bit uncertain about, well, let's say, his identity. You've never told me, Mark, is Mr Potter married?'

Mark, fortunately, hardly heard her. He was standing by the window in a kind of dream, not thinking about anything. He fiddled with the curtain, twitching it open, then shut, then open again. Perhaps he touched the dark pane. When he looked again there was a word written in condensation on the glass. A name.

'Mum,' he said. 'Who's Lucy?'

The tea went everywhere, on the quilt, over his mother's cords, on the carpet. She said he had jogged her arm and Mark, dabbing frantically, was not in any position to argue. But when she was downstairs again, safely in front of the television, he looked sideways at her face and saw she was still afraid. He wanted to ask her again, 'Who's Lucy?' but he didn't dare.

CHAPTER FIVE

Mark was one of the last to reach the classroom for the first lesson, French, next morning. Miss Sturgiss hadn't arrived yet and the classroom was locked, so all the girls were leaning against the wall outside, chatting and watching the boys. Craig and Graham were kicking someone's bag around, showing off. Mark went over to the window and stood by himself, looking out. He didn't want to have to talk to anybody. The air of the corridor was warm and stale and though the day had hardly started he already felt tired. His mother had put the radio on the table along with the breakfast things; there had been no opportunity to talk and anyway, what could he say to her? She wouldn't let him do music now, however much he pleaded. He had given in, and that was that.

He stared out at the fine blue sky and wished he was somewhere else, living in a bus or a caravan maybe, like the tattered boys who sat around the shopping centre in town, drinking cans of beer and playing with their dogs. Some of them were no older than him. They took things out of skips and did odd jobs and looked after themselves. He could do that. He could play his trumpet in the street and get money and someone would come along and discover him, and pay to send him to music college. His head full of it, he swung open the window and leant out, breathing in a deep lungful of cold fresh air. The wind stirred his hair and chilled his face, and he felt free. He leant further out, releasing his shoulders, then his arms; his legs were stretched and his belt scraped on the sill. He wanted to be outside. He swung his arms in the empty air and looked past the faded lines on the tarmac playground, the battered netball hoops and the scuffed grass, beyond the fence and the dirty white houses, as far as the trees of the park. Abruptly he pulled in, back inside, almost knocking into someone beside him in his hurry. It was Claire Savage, the girl he sat next to in music.

'Get a grip,' she said impatiently. 'Sturgiss hasn't arrived yet, you know.' Then, looking at him more closely, she added, 'What's the matter with you, anyway? You look as if you've seen a ghost.'

Mark didn't know Claire very well, but he liked her. She was small and quick and thin, not exactly pretty, but with nice creamy skin and short dark hair that curled into the nape of her neck. She had never made fun of him, and always called him by his given name.

'Do you believe in ghosts?' he asked her cautiously.

She thought for a moment, treating the question as seriously as she did most things. 'I don't know. Why, do you think you've seen one?'

'Maybe,' Mark said. He didn't know whether he could trust her. 'I saw something in the park,' he said impulsively. 'Now I think it's got into our house. It wrote a name on the window.'

'A name?' She looked puzzled. 'What name?'

'Lucy.'

She grinned suddenly. 'Well, if it is a ghost, you'll have to stop calling her "it".'

'What do you mean?' Mark said stupidly.

In the abrupt silence that greeted Miss Sturgiss's arrival, she whispered it to him. 'If it's Lucy, it must be a *she*.'

Mark had a seat by himself in the front row, next to a large poster of the Eiffel Tower. Behind him, in a buzz of talk, bags were dumped on and off desks, books retrieved and chairs scraped into comfortable positions. Mark found the right page in his own book, folded his arms and tried to look as keen as usual, but his heart wasn't in it. Neither, it seemed, was Miss Sturgiss's.

'Right then,' she said, unenthusiastically, 'let's get started, shall we?' She began writing on the board with a squeaky marker pen. 'Who remembers what we were doing before the test? Claire? How do you say "Can you tell me the way to the station, please?"'

'*Pour aller à la gare*, Miss?'

'Almost. What has she left out,

Khalida?'

'*S'il vous plaît*, Miss.'

'That's right. Very important to mind your Ps and Qs in French, or in any other language.'

As soon as she turned from the board, Mark shot up his hand. 'Please, Miss, have you marked our test yet?'

Miss Sturgiss looked harassed. 'No, Mark, not yet. Not everybody's as anxious as you are to know their results, I imagine.'

There was a titter from the class and a loud guffaw from Craig, sitting at the back. 'Bet you don't know why he's so anxious to get his marks, Miss. He writes them all down in a little book, and takes them out to look at when he's depressed. That's what he gets off on, the little swot.'

'It is not!' Mark swung round in his seat indignantly. He turned red as the boys at the back around Craig started to laugh. 'I mean, I never write my marks in a book,' he said hotly and untruthfully. 'Whoever told you that's a liar, Craig Moran.'

'Oh, Tim Wilson's a liar, is he?' Craig

retorted coolly. 'I'll tell him you said that.'

'Tim Wilson's a wanker and so are you,' Mark said, furious.

'Mark Robson!' Miss Sturgiss was shocked. 'That's hardly the language I expect you to use in class.'

'You should hear him outside school, Miss,' Craig said sorrowfully.

'I don't want to hear either of you in my lesson, unless it's speaking French,' Miss Sturgiss said severely.

Graham put up his hand. 'What *is* the French for wanker, Miss?' he asked politely. 'I mean, can you just say "*vous êtes absolument un grand wankeur*"?'

'And is there a verb for it, Miss?' Craig asked.

'A regular verb it would have to be for Porker,' Graham said. '*Je wanks, tu wanks, il wank...*'

'*Voulez-vous un wank, Porceur?*' enquired Craig.

They only shut up properly when Miss Sturgiss threatened to send them to Mr Moynihan.

As the rest of the class launched into an enquiry about buses to Grenoble,

Mark sneaked a look along the row of desks towards Claire. She pulled a sympathetic face at him, and he sat back, surprised to feel so happy. When the bell rang, he lingered over putting his things away, but when he went out into the corridor, she was waiting.

'They're pigs,' she said at once, 'and you should just ignore them. That's all you can do, really. They'll pick on anyone. They call Khalida a Paki cow, and Nicky a spastic because of his legs. What I mean is, it's not you. It's them, the ignorant lot.'

Mark was so surprised he couldn't think of anything much to say. He asked her hurriedly, 'Are you going down to the cloakrooms? We could walk together, if you like.'

She nodded, and he set off with her towards the stairs, not speaking, but thinking how nice she was, how nice her hair smelt. Her sleeve brushed his when they reached the swing door, but he got there just in time and swept it open for her.

'How do you know I'm not a feminist?' she said, a bit crossly, which

68

made him worry he had done the wrong thing, but when they reached the bottom of the stairs, she touched his arm to stop him. 'Look—' she said, hesitated, then went on quickly. 'They have to pick on you for something, so they find whatever they can. Do you remember, my little brother started here last year?'

Mark nodded. He vaguely remembered him, quite a small boy with scared rabbit eyes.

'They gave him the full treatment,' Claire said, rather bitterly. 'Stole his dinner money, shoved him around, the lot. They couldn't find anything else to pick on, so they called him a poof. My dad decided to take him away from the school in the end and send him to Grangepark High, which was against his principles, really. He always votes Labour.'

Mark nodded intelligently. Grangepark High was a private school, a good one. Mark sometimes wished *his* parents had the money to carry out their Tory principles properly.

'All I'm saying is, they pick on whatever they can. Martin Devlin's just as large as you are, if you look, but nobody makes a big deal out of it with him.'

Mark looked at her dumbly. He was now certain she was the most wonderful girl he had ever met, but not a word could he find to utter in reply.

'Will you be coming over to the music block this lunch time?' she asked. She played the viola in the school orchestra, of course. Mark had often seen her in the music room, practising properly, not chatting and messing about like the other girls.

'No, not today,' he said with regret. He hadn't bothered to bring his trumpet to school today. There hadn't seemed any point. They looked at each other awkwardly.

'See you around, then,' said Claire.

'See you,' Mark echoed reluctantly.

She walked off in the direction of the girls' cloakroom. 'Let me know about the ghost,' she called back over her shoulder.

'I will,' he promised.

A little later, he walked into the hall, feeling very happy. Usually it embarrassed him to buy something to eat at break, but after what Claire had just said, he thought he had as much right as anyone. He felt in his pocket for some change and crossed the hall towards the vending machines in the alcove. The last person he expected to see was Tim. He was sitting in his usual place on a stack of dinner tables, shoulders hunched, hands in his pockets, quite alone. Mark's instinct was to ignore him. He walked up to one of the machines, fed in his money and extracted a giant cookie, feeling as self-conscious as if he was being filmed. As he tore open the cellophane wrapper with his teeth, Tim behind him said, 'Hello, Mark.'

Mark turned round. Tim was standing close by, smiling uncertainly. 'Hello,' Mark said, keeping it cold and short. 'Who are you waiting for? Craig, I suppose.'

'No, they've gone down the shops for some cigarettes. I didn't feel like going.'

'You were scared of getting caught, you mean,' Mark said, and laughed.

Tim's smile wavered and went out. 'I can't win with you, can I?' he said with

71

surprising bitterness. 'If I do anything with them, I'm a delinquent, and if I don't, I'm a coward. Brilliant.'

'I don't care what you do,' Mark said. 'I don't know what you expect from me anyway; a round of applause?'

Tim hunched his shoulders and looked away, muttering about it being a waste of time trying to talk to some people.

'Oh, for goodness' sake,' Mark said, exasperated by Tim's look of misery. 'Have a bit of this cookie and stop moaning.' He held it out and Tim broke a bit off, turning it round and round in his hand before putting it into his mouth. There was a pause, filled with the noise of Tim crunching and swallowing.

'Thanks,' he said when he had finished. 'Well—thanks.'

Neither of them seemed to know how to proceed. Tim scuffed one shoe against the other and coughed, and Mark fiddled with the top button of his shirt under his tie. They couldn't quite manage to meet each other's eyes. The silence lasted until Mark's most pressing grievance spilled into speech.

'You know, you needn't have told Craig about my results book,' he said angrily. 'That was supposed to be private. I only told you because we were friends.'

Tim looked uncomfortable. 'I didn't want to. But you don't know what Craig's like. You have to keep telling him things just to stay in with him.'

'Great,' Mark nodded. 'Sounds terrific, Tim. I can just see why you packed me in for him.'

Tim's eyes were on his feet, digging at the parquet floor. 'I told you why before, Mark. You just wouldn't listen. You just got upset.'

'All right,' Mark said tightly. 'Tell me now.'

Tim sighed, and delivered one last hack to the floor before looking up. 'Craig's popular,' he began unwillingly. 'He can go round with anyone he likes. So if he wants to go round with me, it means something, doesn't it? It's a compliment. He must like me. Whereas you only go round with me because you have to, because there isn't anyone else.'

'That's not true,' Mark said, fiercely.

73

'I've got other people I can go round with. One of them's a girl, as a matter of fact.'

If Tim was impressed, he didn't show it. 'What I meant was, you don't really like me,' he said.

'Yes, I do,' Mark said, and blushed.

'No, you don't,' Tim said. 'I know you don't.'

There was a horrible silence.

'You'd think,' Mark said eventually, staring at a point above Tim's head, 'you'd think it'd mean something how upset I got when you went off with Craig.'

Tim blinked and scratched his leg with sudden violence. 'But you never listened to a word I said when we went round together,' he complained. 'You never wanted to do any of the things I liked.'

'Look who's talking,' Mark retorted. 'I don't remember you being phenomenally responsive when I was trying to explain to you how the Stock Exchange works.'

Tim muttered something desperate and gazed away around the hall.

'Look,' said Mark, and stopped. He

was burning inside and he knew he would look back at this with the most horrible embarrassment, but he also knew it had to be said. 'Look, Tim, I've really missed going round town with you, and that. Hanging round here at break, and up in your room, whatever. The thing is, however much we get on each other's nerves, you're still my best friend, and you probably always will be.'

Tim said nothing. He bent down to pick up the cellophane wrapper Mark had dropped and batted it towards the bin. The tips of his ears, Mark saw, burned with a glowing red. When he straightened up he gave an embarrassed cough.

'Actually, it's not so brilliant being with Craig and them,' he admitted. 'I get a bit sick of it at times.'

'I can believe it,' Mark said.

'What I'm trying to say is,' Tim coughed again, loudly, 'if you're not doing anything one evening, if you're at a loose end, kind of, you could always call round.'

'Thanks,' Mark said. 'Really, thanks, Tim.'

They were both rather embarrassed now, and it was a relief when the bell rang for the next lesson.

'I'll have to get a move on,' Mark said quickly. 'We've got maths with Buddha Brown and you know what he's like.'

Tim nodded. 'I'll probably have to stay with them at break tomorrow,' he said, looking at Mark rather anxiously. 'Don't—don't let it wind you up if you see me with them, all right?'

'Course I won't,' Mark said cheerfully. 'I shall just have to be careful when I come round to your house, though, won't I?' He picked up his bag and skidded across the polished floor to the door, grinning back at Tim before he plunged into the scrum outside.

When he got home that afternoon, he didn't want to go in. All the good things that happened, happened somewhere else.

CHAPTER SIX

The next day at lunch time, Mark went into the music block, trumpet case in hand. He spotted Claire at once. She was standing near the window in the corridor, with her music propped up on the window sill, bowing with concentration. Her back was to him, and he was too unsure of his welcome to go across and interrupt. Instead he went on towards the classroom, glancing in at the window to see who was there. This proved to be a bad move; Mr Potter, standing just inside the door, spotted him and waved him in.

'Mark, Mark,' he said. 'Come and look at this. It's for the first years this afternoon. Do you think they'll make sense of it?'

Mark moved forward reluctantly. There was a little group of girls from his own year gathered near the board, gazing admiringly at Mr Potter as he went into action again, thick blond hair flopping across his forehead as he wrote.

Mark found the girls very stupid and irritating; didn't they know Mr Potter was a serious man? And anyway, he was married.

'Looks all right to me,' he said aloud. It was only simple things about bass and treble clefs and note values, kid's stuff.

'Good. That's finished with,' Mr Potter said, wiping his hands on his jacket. 'All right girls, back to work. You're allowed up here to practise, you know, not to mess about.'

They dispersed reluctantly, back to the abandoned clarinets and recorders laid down on desks around the room. As the squeaks and scales and fragments of melody resumed around them, Mr Potter smiled at Mark and said, 'Have you asked your parents yet about doing music next year?'

Mark dropped his eyes and stared at Mr Potter's scuffed desert boots. 'Not yet,' he said.

'Don't look so worried,' Mr Potter said comfortingly. 'You've got a bit of time yet.'

'I s'pose.'

'But I do want you in next year's class,

you know. I think it would be a great waste if you gave up music now. You can tell your mother I said so.'

Mark looked up and felt the familiar jump of the heart, a small shock of pleasure and panic as he met Mr Potter's eyes. 'I was practising the Berlioz last night,' he said, almost in a gabble. 'You know, the second entry where I always come in too soon. I think I've got it right now. It's just a question of counting the rests properly, like you said.'

'Good,' said Mr Potter cheerfully. 'We can't have you coming in wrong during the concert. You're one of our star performers.'

'Thanks,' Mark said.

Mr Potter looked at him. 'Are you all right? You seem a bit down. Nothing wrong at home, is there?'

Mark couldn't tell him. He willed Mr Potter to know, to guess; but Mr Potter only smiled and waited.

'Oh, it's nothing,' Mark said eventually. 'I'll sort it out.' As he spoke, he moved towards the door. 'Actually, there's someone I have to see now,' he added, and quickly made his escape.

Once outside in the foyer, Mark dumped his trumpet case down on a bench and sat down beside it. Over by the window, Claire stopped playing and turned round.

'I thought I saw your reflection,' she said. 'Have you come to practise?'

'I was going to,' Mark said. 'I don't feel like it now.'

Claire came over, holding her viola and bow. 'What's up?'

'Oh, it's complicated,' Mark said. He wished she knew all about it already; he felt too shy and too sick of it all to start explaining.

Claire studied him, evidently thinking. 'How's the ghost?' she said lightly, after a bit.

'I don't know.' Mark was glad to think about something else. 'I sort of listened out for it last night when I went to bed, but there wasn't anything. Not in my room, anyway.'

'Lucy,' Claire said. 'Lucy. Do you know of any Lucys in your family?'

'It's my grandmother's name,' Mark said. 'But it can't be anything to do with her. For one thing, she's still alive.'

Claire grinned. 'Not a good candidate, then.'

'No,' Mark said, cheering up a bit. 'But you know, it's not exactly like a traditional ghost at all. I mean, it started off in the park. Now it's in the house. But there's no form to it. It's just a feeling. It could all be in my head.'

'But the name was written on the window,' Claire said.

'My mum thinks I did that.' Mark remembered the look she had given him. 'I could have. Maybe I did it without knowing. I certainly don't remember writing it.'

'Have you asked her who Lucy is?'

'She won't tell me,' Mark said. 'But I think she knows. In fact, I'm sure she does.'

Claire frowned. 'Well, why not ask her again, then? I mean, it's a simple enough question.'

'You don't know my mother,' Mark said.

Claire thoughtfully prodded her toes with her bow. 'If it's like that, you'll just have to find out some other way,' she said.

'Yeah?' Mark waited for her to suggest one, but she didn't. Instead she continued, 'You know, it could be telepathy, something you're picking up from someone else's mind. Or the imprint of something that's actually happened. My dad's very interested in finding scientific evidence for things like that. He's a psychologist.'

'Oh, really?' Mark was both daunted and impressed. 'What does your mother do?' he asked, hoping it would be something more ordinary, like working in a sweet shop.

Claire's face stiffened. 'She doesn't live with us. She lives with someone called Kelvin, who lectures on brick technology at the poly. Something like that. She works in the accommodation office. That's how they met.'

'Oh, I see,' Mark said, rather shocked.

'You think you see, but you don't,' Claire said. 'I'm glad Mum went. It took her eighteen months of agonising, going backwards and forwards between us and him. I'm surprised old Kelvin waited. By the end of it, she and Dad couldn't be in the same room without screaming at each other. Things are better as they are. At least it's quiet and we all know what's happening. And I see her, and everything.' She pulled a face. 'So what are your parents like?'

'Average,' Mark said, disloyally. 'About C-minus, I suppose.'

'My dad's A-plus,' Claire said fiercely. 'He's brilliant. You should see him cook spaghetti. Stripy apron, bottle of wine— just like that guy on the telly. I just wish he had better taste in girlfriends.'

'Is he going to let you do music?' Mark asked, involuntarily.

'Let me?' Claire stared. 'What do you mean, let me? It's up to me to choose what I want to do.'

'Well, then, are you?' Mark asked. 'Is music going to be one of your options?'

'Yup.'

'Same here,' Mark said. 'At least, it will be if I can sort it out.' He took a breath. 'My mum's not very sympathetic.'

'It's your life,' Claire said.

Mark wanted to hug her. 'It is,' he said, and then he laughed. 'Will you come and tell my mum that?'

'If you like,' Claire said. She tapped him lightly on the head with her bow. 'You shouldn't need me to do it, though.'

'I don't, really,' Mark said quickly. 'I'm going to do music whatever she thinks about it.' As he spoke he wondered how he could possibly make that true.

*   *   *

When he got home that evening he realised to his relief that both his parents were out. It was one of his mother's evenings for working late at the supermarket, and his father had probably taken the opportunity to go to the pub. In the kitchen the tea was laid out, individual portions of lasagne and a chocolate swiss roll for pudding. Mark put his lasagne in the oven and went into the living room to watch the cartoons. He sat on the settee hugging his knees; he was tired of thinking and just wanted to lose himself in the nonsense on the screen. He remembered the lasagne just in time. He ate it out of the foil container with a tablespoon, then sat back again, flipping channels to avoid the news. He had started to do his homework on the coffee table when he heard his father come in and walk unsteadily down the hall towards the kitchen. Mark was glad when it became clear he meant to stay there. He watched television and wrote up his science notes until it grew nearer and nearer to the time when his mother was due back. The closer it got, the more nervous he became. He decided that after all it wasn't a good idea to raise the question of music with her, not after a long day when she would be tired and irritable. Yesterday evening had been terrible, full of angry silence over Lucy. Just before nine o'clock, Mark packed up his books and went upstairs.

He got undressed and began to read an old tattered paperback about King Arthur and his knights that he had last read when he was about eleven. When he heard his mother come in he switched off the light, though it was still early. He lay in the dark and after a few minutes he heard her come upstairs. She knocked softly on his door. She even called to him. Mark held his breath until he heard her step quietly away.

He woke in the night and the fear was back. He could feel it like an animal in the room, squatting on the bed, breathing. The house was quiet and the street light shone through the gap in the curtains and outlined the familiar furniture. Through the wall he could hear deep regular snoring. He lay still for a few minutes, then threw off the covers and stood up. The fear rose with him, making him giddy for a moment, as if he was going to faint. He picked up his trumpet case and took out his trumpet. He felt better holding it. His fingers moved on the valves, playing ghost scales. Still the fear. He opened the door, and, trumpet in hand, padded down the landing to the spare room. It was warm in there, warm and friendly in the dark. He opened the curtain and saw a high small moon, up in the left corner. It lit enough of the window for him to see the writing. The window was covered with the name Lucy, written over and over in large straggling letters.

'Lucy,' he said aloud. 'What's the

matter? Are you the one that's so afraid?' There was no answer. 'Was it you in the park?'

Mark had a sudden conviction that she was outside the window, outside in the cold and the dark. He pushed up the window, but there was only air and darkness, a car moving away and a dog barking in the next street. Leaning out of the window, he began to play the trumpet, softly at first, then louder. Fear shook his mouth and his hands, making him play badly, and he felt more ordinary embarrassment as lights winked on in bedrooms down the street. Nevertheless, he played on. He felt sure Lucy could hear him.

Suddenly the light went on behind him and he felt hard fingers on his shoulder, pulling him in. It was his mother. Dressed in a pale green cotton nightie, she looked skinny and unkempt. Her hair was flattened, with odd bits sticking up, and her face was creased and bleary with sleep.

'What do you think you're doing?' she demanded, furious. 'You'll wake the dead with that racket!' She pushed him away from the window and banged it down. Then she saw the writing and her face changed.

'Who is Lucy?' Mark said urgently. 'You've got to tell me.'

His mother didn't answer. She was looking at the writing, the big crooked letters. Her hand went to her mouth. For a moment she just stood there, then she made a fist and violently rubbed the letters away. She pulled the curtains to, and turned to face Mark, white with rage and resentment.

'I don't know why you're doing this,' she said.

A cold trickle of perspiration ran down the back of Mark's neck. 'It's not me,' he said. 'Don't say it's me. It's Lucy. It's been Lucy all along. It was Lucy in the park.'

His mother closed her eyes. Her face squeezed together as if something heavy was pressing it down. 'I don't want to hear it!' Opening her eyes, she added more calmly, 'I suppose you've been poking about in our things. Or maybe someone's said something. I don't know, and I don't want to know. What you have to understand, Mark, is this. We went through it, me and your dad, and we decided it's not your business. That's what we decided a long time ago, and that's what we're sticking to, all right?' She tried, unsuccessfully, to smile. 'It's not so bad, is it? You know I only want the best for you. And we've got a nice family, haven't we, just you and me and your dad? We have a nice enough time, don't we?'

Mark only looked at her.

'Oh, go to bed,' she said, suddenly tired of it. 'You'll apologise in the morning.'

But Mark didn't. In the morning, after she had gone to work, he set off with his school bag to the park.

CHAPTER SEVEN

The weather had changed. It was dull and cold, with a raw touch of fog that caught the throat and chilled through layers of clothing. Mark stopped outside the front door to put on his gloves before

89

walking down to the main road. It was clogged with cars edging into town and there were long queues at the bus stops for buses stranded in the heavy traffic. Some of the shops were already open. As Mark reached the general store on the corner, its Pakistani owner came out and started doing something to the crates of fruit and vegetables stacked outside. Mark passed him with some embarrassment. His father sometimes bought whisky there, but his mother wouldn't go near the place. She claimed that the smell of curry got into everything they sold, even the biscuits, and she didn't like to see babies playing on the floor where she had to shop.

Further down the road Mark saw two girls from his school. He kept his distance. When they crossed the road at the traffic lights, he dodged behind a parked car to stay out of sight. Till then he had pretended to himself that he was just going to school as usual. Now, as he cautiously moved down the street, he avoided the eyes of adults. He found himself explaining inside his head that he didn't skip school as a habit, that he was going to the park because he had to. He felt ridiculously conspicuous, as if everyone around him must know. The park was in sight now, and beyond it, the turning that led to his school. Mark had forgotten about the lollipop man stationed on the road just outside the park gates. Flocks of small children gathered on the pavement to be escorted across the road by him. The older ones, Mark's contemporaries, preferred to risk the traffic further down, but Mark still felt in danger. Someone was sure to see him, a parent who knew his mother, or someone from his school escorting a little brother or sister. He stopped on the pavement, bent down and untied and retied his laces, trying to think. As he straightened up, a wave of children surged over the pavement round him towards the crossing. Mark moved after them. The old man in his white mackintosh planted his lollipop firmly in the middle of the road and waved them across. On the other side, Mark took a quick look round, gripped his bag hard and ducked into the park.

No one had noticed him. No one

shouted a protest. The silence in the memorial garden was startling after the roar of traffic outside. He walked down the gravel path past the sodden bushes and, skirting the playground, took another path that led between sloping lawns to the lake. The grass was wet and among the distant trees there was a white thickening of the air. No one was in sight on the path or the wide, wet lawns. In a corner near a rockery he saw tools and a wheelbarrow, but no gardener. He reached the trees and bushes near the lake, then the path bent round suddenly and he came upon an occupied bench. At a second glance Mark realised the man sitting there was a tramp. He sat hunched forward, his thin hair flattened against his scalp and the shoulders of his torn raincoat stained with wet. He was muttering to himself. When he coughed it sounded like the deep bark of an animal. He paid no heed as Mark edged past.

He had reached the boathouse. The dull green front was shuttered, a faded notice on the door listing the prices for boats and for the nearby putting green.

Mark went over and studied it, then looked at the boats and the brown lake. He was in no hurry now. The place where he had seen the little patch of darkness was just ahead, between the water's edge and the path. His chest felt tight and the muscles of his body felt tense and weak. He told himself not to be afraid. He picked up his bag and advanced round the side of the boathouse.

There was nothing there. Ordinary mud and brown lake water squatted under the trees.

'Lucy,' Mark whispered, and then more loudly, 'Lucy!'

But there was nothing. He wanted to tear at the dull sky showing between black branches, uproot the path, insist on her presence. He watched the place until his eyes were sore and swimming, but it made no difference. There was nothing there. Eventually it began to drizzle, pocking the water and tapping on the boathouse roof. That somehow put an end to it. He turned slowly and made his way to the gate.

Outside in the street the air smelt of petrol. The lollipop man had gone and the traffic was moving smoothly. Mark could not face school. He turned back along the main road towards home. The drizzle had thickened into rain by the time he reached the house and he was clumsy with haste trying to fit his key into the lock. He struggled inside with his bag. The hall, being dry, felt welcoming. He called out, 'Dad?' just in case, but there was no answer so he went through to the kitchen and hung his wet coat on the back of a chair.

He sat down and took off his shoes. Mum always made him have a hot drink after being in the wet, but the gleaming stove and empty washing-up bowl did not encourage it. Everything was in its place except him. He glanced up at the clock. Ten to ten. He was missing double history with Miss Rogers. He tried to suppress the feeling that she knew he was there in the kitchen, but the silence made him feel uncomfortable and he got up and put on the radio. A woman's voice filled a corner of the room with an argument about government spending cuts.

Mark, after a minute's distraction,

came to sudden focus. If Mum knew who Lucy was, then there could be evidence in the house. What had she said last night? *You must have been going through our things.* Something like that. Then there was something to find. Still he hesitated. It didn't seem quite right, and yet what was he supposed to do if she wouldn't tell him anything? Claire had said almost the same; there were other ways of finding out. And he had to know. He went out into the hall and climbed the stairs quickly, two at a time.

He didn't often enter his parents' room and it felt strange to open the door and go inside. It was more or less as he remembered it. The bed, covered in a sagging blue crocheted bedspread, took up half the room. The wallpaper, painted the colour of magnolia, was stained above the bed where his father leaned his head against the wall. There were no pictures or ornaments. Next to the door was the crammed wardrobe with its door leaning permanently open. Stacked on top were the family's suitcases. Mark could not remember the last time they had been taken down.

He went over to the dressing table in the bay window. The top was dusty with his mother's talc. He pulled a face at himself in the mirror, then looked at his parents' wedding photograph, stuck in one corner behind the body lotion. His father was caught with his head back and his eyes half-closed, looking young and pink in a dark suit and wide striped tie. His mother stared straight into the camera, clutching his arm. She looked a stranger in her lacy dress and long dark hair.

Mark left them to it and knelt down to open the bottom drawer. Here his mother kept the family photograph album and wallets of loose pictures, along with Mark's old school reports, his poems and drawings from primary school and more embarrassing relics of his babyhood, his first shoes, a front tooth, and a lock of fine brown hair. He ignored the album and the wallets of photographs. He knew what they contained. His mother had brought them downstairs to show him many times. His hand slid underneath them, groping to the bottom of the drawer. But all he fetched up were loose photographs of himself aged about three, struggling with a watering can in his grandparents' back garden, and a hazy snap of his grandmother, frowning at the camera. He left the drawer and tried the bedside cabinets. In his mother's there was a packet of mints, a puzzle book and a knitting pattern; in his father's an empty miniature bottle of Bell's. Mark sat back on his heels, defeated.

Maybe it was all in his head. Maybe he was mad and his mother was right and they were a nice happy family.

'You've got to help me, Lucy,' he said aloud, feeling a fool. 'If you want me to find it, show me where to look.'

He got to his feet and stared round the room. Only the wardrobe was left. The gaping door irritated him, and he went over to it, intending to look inside and then bang it shut. Above the hanging rail there was a shelf where his father kept sweaters and scarves. Mark reached up and felt under the bottom layer of sweaters, and his hand knocked against something hard. He had hardly had time to register that it might be a photograph frame, when he pulled it out and turned it over. A small girl smiled up at him. She had short fair hair cut straight across her forehead and she had lost one of her front teeth. She was wearing a blue-checked summer dress, like the girls who went to the local Catholic primary school. Mark stared at her. He knew and he did not know.

He walked out of his parents' room and crossed the landing. In the spare room he sat down on the bed and placed the photograph on the white chest of drawers. As soon as he had done it he realised. This was her room. It was a little girl's room. She was his sister.

'Lucy?' he said. And she was there, not darkness, not a ghost, but absorbed and happy, playing on the floor near his feet. He could see nothing, but he knew she was there.

'Lucy, what happened to you?'

She played on, unaware of him. Small sounds reached him, and he thought he could make out the outlines of toy animals. The warmth of her filled the room. And suddenly she turned and he saw her face, small chin raised towards him, blue eyes surprised under a straight blonde fringe.

The image was gone as soon as formed, the room empty.

* * *

Downstairs, a man on the television was talking about the geometry of circles. Maths for Schools. Mark stared at him, watching his mouth and hands move. He turned the sound down, then he turned it up again. As he sat down, someone came in, banging the front door. Mark looked round. His father was standing in the open doorway, his fawn raincoat stained with wet and his hair flattened. He looked at Mark uneasily.

'What are you doing back?'

'Dentist.'

'You never said anything about it at breakfast.'

'Didn't I?' Mark said. 'I must have forgotten.'

His father sat down heavily without taking off his coat. Its acrid smell filled the room. 'It was wet out,' he said superfluously. 'So I came back. Caught you out, didn't I?'

'I'm only missing history,' Mark said. 'You won't tell Mum, will you?'

His father smiled faintly. 'I used to bunk off a lot at your age. Couldn't stand school. They were always belting me for it, my dad and the headmaster. But I thought you loved the place.'

'Not really,' Mark said. He turned back to the television and fiddled with the knob, darkening the picture till it was gone. 'Are you happy, Dad?' he asked over his shoulder.

'Happy?' his father repeated. 'What makes you ask that all of a sudden?'

'Because I want to know.'

The settee creaked as his father shifted his weight. 'No, I'm not exactly happy,' he said at last. 'I'm all right, though. We all are, aren't we?'

Mark didn't answer. He turned the knob the other way so that the picture was lost in light.

Behind him, his father said, 'You're in a funny mood, Mark. I hope you're not starting any of that teenage carry-on. Bunking off school, and all that business last night when you should have been in bed. Your mother didn't tell me what that was about and I didn't ask.'

'Why not?' Mark turned round. 'Why didn't you ask?'

His father looked taken aback. 'I leave all that to your mother,' he said.

'I bet you didn't with Lucy.'

His father's face went completely blank. Then colour poured into it, an angry mottled red. He hauled himself out of the settee and made for the door.

'You have to tell me what happened,' Mark shrilled behind him. 'It isn't *fair!*'

His father stopped dead. He turned round, one big hand clutching the door. Mark quailed at his expression. 'Life isn't fair,' he said harshly.

A moment later the front door banged shut.

Proof, said the cold logician lodged in Mark's brain. He fidgeted around the room, picking up ornaments with fingers so nervous he almost dropped them, switching off the television and kicking the rug straight. Then he sat down, picked up a cushion and started to cuddle it, hugging himself into a tight ball. To his own surprise he began to cry, hot, violent and exhausting tears.

CHAPTER EIGHT

When Mark finished crying he stood at the window for a long time, looking out at the rain. He started to feel hungry but it didn't matter. He was too deeply shaken to care. He couldn't think for himself any more; he tried to think instead what Claire would do. It came to him eventually that there was something he could try, but that meant movement, effort, and it was a while before he could summon the necessary energy to go into the kitchen and put on his shoes and his coat.

Outside it was still raining heavily. He walked bare-headed to the bus stop on the main road. When the bus arrived it was full and he had to stand squeezed in between two girls who ducked and bobbed round him to continue their conversation. It took about ten minutes to get into town, and by that time Mark had learnt more than he wanted to know about the sex life of a third girl, apparently their fellow student at the poly.

When they reached the centre, Mark fought his way off the bus with the other passengers and ducked across the road into the shopping mall. This was where he spent most of his Saturday afternoons with Tim. The air was warm, dry and perfumed, the decor was pastel blue and orange, and from hidden speakers there drifted muted Christmas carols played by a string orchestra. Against his will Mark felt soothed and comforted. He walked along the row of open-fronted shops, which had been decorated for so long with Christmas snow and holly that he hardly noticed it any more. All the same he found himself making a mental note to choose cards for Claire and Tim. He bought some cookies from the American Cookie Company, lured by the rich chocolaty smell, and ate them outside the travel shop, inspecting the price of last minute holidays. He picked out a family trip to Crete, 14 days half-board with optional excursions, and moved on to the record shop. The thumping bass of its stereo system wiped out the carols and clashed with the output of the hi-fi shop two doors down.

Mark looked up at the first floor where there was a glass-walled café, full of girls from secretarial college drinking espresso coffee, laughing and sweeping their hair back from their faces. Sometimes, if they had the money, Tim and he used to go there on a Saturday, Tim to examine minutely his purchases of military magazines and glue, and Mark to look at the girls and boys at the other tables, talking and touching each other, singing the words of the songs. He wondered now if Claire had ever been one of them. Then he was filled with a stupid panic that his father might be up there, looking down at him. He told himself not to be an idiot; his father never came into the mall, preferring the cheap place near the library, where he could sit over a cup of tea for hours undisturbed. And now most likely he was in a pub, getting over his rage, or fuelling it.

Mark walked quickly on and reached the square at the end of the line of shops.

Here there was a big circular seat built around an enormous tub of what had once been shrubs and was now mostly litter. The seat was occupied by a group of young homeless, driven in by the rain. They were boys mostly, with one or two girls wearing knitted blankets over torn Indian dresses and big army boots. Their hair was dyed or shaven. The girls looked dirty and unattractive to Mark, but they seemed friendly enough, talking to their dogs and sharing round their cans of lager with the boys. Two blue-shirted security guards stood outside the supermarket with folded arms, watching them narrowly. Straight ahead was the entrance to offices built above the shops. Mark paused to check the board beside the door. A solicitor, an accountant, the secretarial college, and the registry office. Without letting himself think about it, he had reached his destination. He took a bite of his last cookie, stepped inside and summoned the lift.

When he reached the second floor he entered a maze of passages in grey brick and glass. The number of the office he wanted was 43, and he followed the arrows faithfully until he reached a blank wall and the stairs to the multistorey car park. Retracing his steps, he almost bumped into a middle-aged woman stepping out of the lift. Out of sheer helplessness, he followed her and she led him to the registry office. As they entered the lobby, a receptionist popped out at them.

'I need a birth certificate for my son,' the woman said.

'Same here,' said Mark. 'For me, I mean.'

The receptionist gave him a look, and smiled at the woman. 'Room eight, both of you. It's just along the corridor.'

Mark followed the woman into a kind of waiting room. It had dull green papered walls and a stack of magazines on a low table. At one end sat a woman behind a desk. She was wearing a gold blouse that gleamed dully in the artificial light, and an extraordinary pair of spectacles, cherry coloured and all angles, like the kind of toothbrush people buy to reach their back teeth. Mark felt more and more as if he was at a dentist's. He listened carefully to the conversation between her and the woman he had followed from the lift, but it didn't really help him. She, of course, knew the date of her son's birth and it only took a few minutes for the other woman to check it in the register and have a copy of the certificate made out. When she left, Mark went up to the desk.

'I'd like to look at the register of births, please.'

The woman frowned at him over her glasses, making her chin recede even more.

'I'm afraid that isn't allowed.'

Mark was upset. 'Because of my age?'

'No,' said the woman, looking at his school uniform and then, rather pointedly, at her watch. 'It's confidential information. No one is allowed to see it.'

'That woman just now did. You took her to see it.'

The woman in the cherry glasses sighed heavily and folded her arms. '*No* member of the general public is allowed to see the register. All right, sonny? If you want a certificate, tell me the date and place of birth and the name, of course, and I'll check it in the register.'

Mark resented being called sonny very much, but he said as politely as he could, 'I don't know the exact date, I'm afraid, only the name and place. But it'll have been around twenty years ago, I think.'

'Family tree stuff, is it? Something for a school project?'

Mark wriggled. 'Sort of. Yes, that's it,' he added quickly, as the woman looked at him impatiently. She got up and came round the desk.

'Come through,' she said in a resigned voice.

Mark followed her across the corridor to another room, where another woman sat at an identical desk surrounded by identical wallpaper. But in this room there was a metal wall cupboard standing open. The woman in cherry glasses consulted the other one in a low murmur, then turned to Mark.

'I hope this won't take too long,' she said. 'We're a very busy office. The green ones are births, the black ones are deaths, and the red ones are marriages.'

Mark followed her gesture towards the files in the cupboard. 'But you said I couldn't look,' he objected.

'Not at the *register*,' she said impatiently. 'That's the index. If you see the entry you think is correct, we can look it up and give you a copy. But you can't see what's in the register itself. All right?'

She left the office before Mark could reply. He went over to the cupboard and had a look at the files. He felt very self-conscious with the other woman sitting there at her desk, though she was reading some papers and paid no attention to him. The files of births seemed to go back about thirty years as far as he could tell. He took one down at random and began to skim through it, just to make it appear as if he knew what he was doing. Meanwhile he tried to sort out a starting date in his head. He had been born fourteen years ago. He didn't remember Lucy at all, so the picture at home must have been taken either before he was born or when he was very small. Say she was six or seven when it was taken. That meant she had to be five years older than him at least, but not much more than that because his parents were only in their forties now. He put back the file he was holding and took down one for 1971. There were an awful lot of Robsons. When he found two Lucy Robsons, he shut the file with a snap and put it back.

The woman behind the desk said, 'Did you find what you wanted?'

'It doesn't matter,' Mark said. 'It's a very common name.'

He walked out of the office and took the lift down, feeling angry with himself. Part of him thought it had been a stupid idea anyway, and part felt ashamed that he had been too much of a coward to ask for proper help. When he came out into the square, the security guards were arguing with one of the boys in the group around the bench. His hair was in big tangled dreadlocks and he was very thin. As Mark passed him, the boy gave a slight wave and nod of recognition and Mark, quickening his step, realised too late that he did, in fact, know him. He had been one of the friendlier boys among last year's leavers. In the summer he had left home and gone to live in an old bus on unclaimed land at the back of one of the council estates on the edge of town, but this was the first time Mark had seen him since. It was too late to do anything about it now, in any case; he had almost reached the exit.

Once outside the mall, Mark stood under the dripping overhang of a big department store for a minute, then set off quickly through the rain with his head down. He was afraid to examine the extent of his disappointment. He charged between shoppers, trying to manoeuvre down the crowded street. He didn't know where he was going, or what he was going to do. When he reached the end of the main shopping street he stopped and looked around. Across the road was a café. Warm yellow light streamed out of the open door. Mark was attracted by the chocolate-brown façade and the green plants filling the windows. He crossed the road and got closer. Now he could hear the noise of coffee cups and voices, and beyond that, someone playing the piano. He glanced in. The place was crowded. Umbrellas dripped in a stand by the door and the air was full of smoke and friendly talk. He watched a waiter carrying plates loaded with good food, and the savoury smells brought a rush of water into his mouth. He felt in his pocket and his fingers closed on a pound coin. That should be enough, at least for coffee and a rest in the warm. He stepped in, and before he could change his mind a tall youth with acne and a pony tail swooped down on him.

'Just the one, is it?'

Mark nodded shyly.

'You'll have to share, all right?'

Mark agreed it was all right, though it wasn't. He followed the waiter to a table at the back near the kitchen.

'Just coffee, please,' he said nervously before he had even sat down. He wasn't used to places like this. In the café above the record shop you queued for what you wanted at the counter, and then paid for it before you found a table.

As he sat down, the middle-aged couple finishing a late lunch reluctantly made room for him. Waiters banged in and out of the swing doors into the kitchen. The coffee took a long time to arrive and Mark started to feel edgy. All the other people in the café were adults, students or older people, quite a lot of them in couples. Surreptitiously, he undid his school tie and stuffed it into his pocket. The couple at his table moved closer together, murmuring, and he realised to his embarrassment that they were holding hands under the table. It made him feel slightly outraged; they were older than his parents.

His coffee arrived at last and he tried to drink it much too soon, scalding his mouth. It was strong, rather bitter, and there wasn't very much of it. He added extra sugar and went on drinking it in quick gulps, too self-conscious now to linger. Halfway down he checked the bill. Eighty-five pence, a shocking waste of money, considering the coffee at the other place was only sixty and came in a big mug. He refolded the bill and put the pound coin down on top of it. Even if it meant losing the change he wasn't going to try to catch the waiter's eye. He stood up and fastened his coat. As he turned towards the door he heard a familiar voice behind him, 'Well, you are a naughty boy!'

Mark turned round, his heart beating

very fast. It was Win. She was sitting at a table just across from his. He couldn't understand how he missed seeing her when he came in. He forced himself to smile, but Win wasn't fooled.

'Look at his face! Pleased to see me, aren't you, Mark? Come here often on a school day, do you?'

'I've just been to the dentist,' he said, miserably.

Win winked. 'I won't tell on you if you don't tell on me,' she said, grinning.

It was only then Mark realised there was someone with her, a dark-haired man in a jacket and tie, looking far from pleased. There was a wine bottle on the table, two brandy glasses, and a clutter of dishes and crumpled serviettes. Mark smiled uncertainly at Win's friend, but he only managed a curt nod back.

'Oh—' Win's cigarette waved dangerously close to her hair. 'I'd better introduce you two, hadn't I? Mark, this is Peter from Peter Dominic's. That's rather funny, isn't it? Peter from—and Mark's a friend of mine from way back, aren't you, Mark?'

Peter didn't even look at Mark, but

stared at Win in a fixed tense way, as if he was trying to communicate something urgently. Win's eyes widened suddenly and her face lit up with laughter.

'Don't worry, old son, Mark's not supposed to be here himself, so he won't split on us. And he doesn't know anyone to tell even if he wanted to be rotten, which he wouldn't. He's a good kid, aren't you, Mark?'

'I have to get back to the shop,' Peter said, tightly. He drained his coffee cup and took out some notes from his wallet, throwing them down on top of the bill.

'Are you going to phone me?' Win asked, blowing out smoke.

Peter's tight mouth twitched and relaxed into a smile. 'Of course,' he said. 'Tomorrow lunch time. You'll be at home, won't you? Bye, Mark. Nice to have met you.' He walked away between the tables to the door, Win and Mark both watching him until he was out of sight.

'I'd better—' Mark muttered, preparing to go himself, but Win grabbed his arm.

'Don't go,' she said. 'I always hate this

bit, after he's gone. Sit down and have a drink. There's probably a bit left in the bottle.' She shook it to see.

'That's all right,' Mark said. 'I don't really like wine, to be honest. Not unless it's sweet.' He sat down, though. He didn't see what else he could do.

'So now you've met Peter,' Win said. 'He wasn't at his best. Bit uptight, isn't he? But he's a lovely bloke, really. I catch myself wondering what would happen if—you know. But it's best to keep it on a no strings basis, otherwise everything gets so messy. He *says* his wife doesn't care what he gets up to, but he minds her finding out, all right.' Her expression cleared suddenly and she broke into a warm lazy smile. 'You don't know what I'm on about, really, do you? Girls get started earlier than boys, always have.'

'But you're married, Win,' Mark said. He didn't like to show he was shocked. Win laughed.

'You mean you think that should stop me from seeing someone else? It might if I was a different sort of person. Or if Brian was. He started something with one of the secretaries at work, been going

116

on for years. This is my little bit of compensation, that's all. There's not a lot of harm in it, not unless the kids find out, or I let myself get too soppy over him, and I don't think he'll let me do that.' Her laugh this time was uncertain, and she reached for another cigarette.

After she had lit it, she looked at Mark thoughtfully as he sat with his elbows on the table, trying to look as if he had conversations like this all the time.

'I shouldn't have told you,' she said. 'You hadn't even seen me, had you, when you got up to go? Peter's right, I'm an idiot at times. It's just that it struck me as so funny, seeing you here, where we always come. Both of us being where we shouldn't, being naughty. I thought, I won't tell if he won't. And you won't, will you?' She looked at him anxiously. 'I don't want the kids hurt.'

'I wouldn't know who to tell,' Mark said. He didn't feel shocked any more. He felt as if he liked Win more than he ever had, but he also needed to get away from her. He slid off his seat and stood up.

'Quite right,' Win said. 'Time to go. If

I'm not back soon our Tony'll be back from school and wondering where I am.' But she didn't move.

'So long, then,' Mark said. He tried to say something more, couldn't, and walked away.

When he reached the door, he looked back. She was still sitting there, fingering her cropped blonde hair and blowing out smoke. He thought, she's Mum's best friend. I have to ask her. He forced himself to go back to her table. She looked up at him, surprised.

'Did you forget something?'

He wriggled. 'I just wanted to ask you—' He cleared his throat and started again. 'I want you to tell me about Lucy.'

'Your sister?' Win's surprise increased. 'Do you know about her? Your mum said she hadn't told you.'

'She hasn't. She won't. I found something out, and she won't tell me any more.'

Win looked at him doubtfully. 'I don't think I should say anything, then, do you? It's not that I don't want you to know, Mark, it's just, well, you know. Someone else's family. I wouldn't thank your mum for interfering in mine, however well she meant it.'

'I'll tell her, then,' Mark said. Until he spoke, he didn't know how he felt. He wasn't angry, he was furious with disappointment. Win looked at him blankly.

'Tell her what?'

'About you and that man. That Peter. I'll tell her you're seeing him, and then she won't want to know you any more. She won't want to have you in our house.'

Win began to laugh. She laughed on and on, and it had a horrible sound to Mark, as if he had broken something. He was afraid she had suddenly gone mad, and might do something terrible. He fervently wished he could take back what he had said, but it was too late for that. When at last Win stopped laughing and spoke in her normal voice, he was immeasurably relieved.

'Well, aren't you a charmer?' she said. 'But it won't work, old son. Sorry to disappoint you.'

'Why won't it work?' Mark demanded, feeling ashamed of himself.

'Your mum knows about me, always has. We're friends, remember.'

Now Mark was totally confused. 'But she doesn't approve of stuff like that. Even on telly. She doesn't like me to watch it.'

Win laughed. 'And you don't think she ever changes channels once you're out of the room? She has a life of her own, you know, beyond what you see of her. You kids can never grasp that, somehow.'

'It was a stupid thing to try,' Mark said in a low voice. 'Sorry.'

'Forget it,' Win said. Her face brightened. 'Tell you what, Mark, why don't you ask your gran about Lucy? You never know, she might be willing to talk about it.'

'Yeah, I suppose,' Mark said, tiredly. 'It's worth a try.'

Win looked from him to the room beyond. 'Now if I can just catch that waiter's—God, look at the time, but I've got to have a coffee first and get my head together.'

'I'd better go,' Mark said.

'You better had,' Win agreed,

grinning at him. She touched his arm. 'Don't tell your mum I've spoken to you about Peter, all right? She'll only get angry with you. And me for telling you, of course. But if it slips out, don't worry about it. We'll both survive.'

'Okay,' Mark said, liking her. 'See you round at our house sometime,' he added, a little shyly.

'Sure thing,' said Win, and waved her hand at the waiter.

CHAPTER NINE

The old people's home was a long low building of slate-coloured brick on the edge of the town's biggest housing estate. It was set back from the road behind green railings. A path for visitors ran round to the matron's office at the back and a wider walkway with a wheelchair ramp ran from the gate to the front door, bisecting a ragged lawn. The home was called Wheatacres and had a view from certain rooms across a field of wilting saplings that separated the first block of houses from the local shopping centre. When Mark reached it, walking out from town, the rain had stopped and the street lights had come on, casting an unnatural orange glow over the end of the afternoon.

It always depressed him to enter the building. The corridor was full of warm heavy air, smelling of stale dinners and, faintly, of urine. Just opposite the entrance hall was the television lounge where two or three old women sat in the corner, as immobile as their high-winged red vinyl armchairs. The boom of the television followed Mark to the lift. His grandmother's room was on the first floor and when he knocked he heard her moving about for a while before she opened the door. Her hair was untidy and the zip of her skirt was bulging open over her hip. He realised he had interrupted her afternoon rest.

'Oh, it's you.' Her faint flush darkened into annoyance. 'I suppose you've come to tell me your mum can't manage a visit this week.'

'No.' Mark summoned a smile. 'I just came to see you, Gran.'

She held onto the door, looking at him doubtfully. 'It's not my birthday. It's only just December, so it can't be for Christmas.'

'*Gran*,' Mark protested. 'You know I come more often than that.'

She let out a small long-suffering sigh, and opened the door wide for him to come in.

Her room was small and very warm, but despite the heat she wore a woollen cardigan over her yellow blouse. Mark sat down by the window in an armchair while she eased herself back onto the bed. A stroke had left one arm uselessly folded across her body and her movements were laborious and ungainly. Mark looked away until she had shifted her legs into a comfortable position and tugged down her skirt. On the windowsill was a clock, a postcard he had sent her on a school day trip to the Lakes last summer, and a pile of library books. He glanced at the cover of the top one. It showed a blonde girl in black lacy underwear sprawling on a marble floor with a pool of blood round her head and a crucifix clutched in one hand. It seemed a bit lurid, especially considering the way she went on about violence in society.

'Tell your mother they need changing.'

'What, Gran?'

'The books,' she said impatiently. 'I've read them all.'

'Oh, right.' Mark put down the top one a little guiltily and looked at her. She was settled now, leaning back against the pillows. You could see she was his father's mother. She had the same large features and heavy nose, very plain on an old woman, and, in her case, topped with an incongruous mop of white curls.

'And how is everybody?' she asked. 'Everything all right at home?'

'Yeah.' Mark found himself twisting in his seat to look out of the window. 'Everything's fine.'

'Oh, good.' She sounded almost disappointed. 'So you've nothing to tell me, eh?'

'Not really,' Mark said.

There followed a pause, during which he tried to find a way to begin. His grandmother showed her boredom with a variety of sighs and finger-tapping.

'Well, they're not starving you, are they?' she said eventually. 'You're bigger every time I see you.' Stung, Mark turned to look at her. But her eyes were innocent enough. 'Your father was a big lad, too, at your age,' she went on. 'Stood him in good stead at school. No one gave him any trouble.'

'No one gives me any trouble, either,' Mark retorted, and pulled a threatening face at himself in the mirror.

'Glad to hear it,' said his grandmother. 'Speaking of school, I had some girls come round to see me. They were from your school, weren't they? They said it was history, but I told them it wasn't, not while you're still alive it isn't, it's your life. Anyway, they asked me a lot of questions about how I thought things had changed. They recorded it all on a tape recorder. No messing about with pens and paper for them. Did they tell you about it?' Her face wore the look of cunning it had at Christmas when she was cheating at Monopoly.

'I heard what you said, if that's what you mean,' Mark told her. She had the

125

grace to look a little embarrassed. 'But you needn't worry. No one else knew you were my gran. They mixed all the comments together. In fact,' he decided to rub it in a bit, 'I don't suppose anyone paid much attention to what you said. There was lots of more interesting stuff, about the War and everything. That's what they were really looking for.'

His grandmother felt in her bag for a mint and popped it into her mouth without saying anything. Mark, seizing his advantage, went on, 'But if Mum had heard what you said she would have been furious. Anybody'd think she never came to see you! All that stupid stuff you said about the uncaring society, and people not caring about their families any more.'

'Stupid, was it?' She looked at him with big eyes and made a loud sucking noise with her mint.

'You know it was stupid, Gran,' Mark said. 'You're here because—well, because of your arm, and because Mum has to go out to work and there'd be no one at home to take care of you. Mum says we should be very grateful they managed to offer you a place here, because there's such a big demand.'

'*She* can be grateful,' his grandmother said. 'I'm certainly not.'

Mark looked at her.

'Since you're asking,' she said, in an unnecessarily loud voice, 'I know whose idea this place was. *He'd* have had me at home. I know my son. It was her idea to leave me to die among a load of care-assistants.'

'You're not going to die, Gran,' Mark said, uncomfortably.

'Oh, I'm immortal now, am I?' she snapped. 'That's handy.'

'She comes to see you every week,' Mark said.

'She does. I'm not denying, she's very dutiful. She changes my library books and does my bit of shopping for me, but duty's all it is. There's no kindness in it. And you needn't look at me like that, Mark, because you started this conversation. I'm entitled to say what I think, even if I do draw a pension.'

'I never said you weren't,' Mark muttered, sullenly.

They sat through another silence, his

127

grandmother crunching on her mint.

'Well, what about Dad?' Mark burst out suddenly. 'What about him? Why does he get off all the time when he never does anything for anybody?'

His grandmother's face became very still and sad. 'I remember what he was like,' she said. 'Before the whisky and everything. You can't judge him because you don't know.'

'No one'll tell me, you mean,' Mark said, but not loud enough, because she only looked at him blankly.

'Aren't you missing your tea?'

'What, Gran?' It was so far from his thoughts that by the time he had worked out what she had said, she had repeated it.

'Aren't you missing your tea? It's gone five o'clock.'

'Mum's on late,' he said, not able to remember if it was true or not. He was too tired. On his way to the home he had thought out a vague idea for asking about Lucy, working towards it through something about family photographs and lost relatives, but now he just blurted it out. 'I want to know about Lucy,

Gran, but they won't tell me anything.'

His gran showed no surprise. She nodded, as if she had been waiting for this for years.

'I always knew that was wrong,' she said. 'I always knew that was wrong.' She shut her eyes suddenly and when she opened them, Mark saw tears. He didn't dare speak, but waited for her to go on.

'That was your mother's idea, of course,' she said after a while. 'A fresh start for the new baby, she said. It sounded very convincing, but things don't work like that, do they? People need to know why things are the way they are. Children need things explained.' She looked at him truculently. 'Well, I couldn't tell you myself, could I? Not when you were small. It wasn't my business to interfere. But I promised myself if you ever asked when you were older, then I would.'

'And?' Mark said, trying not to sound impatient.

She paused to consider. 'Your mother never really hit it off with Lucy, somehow. It happens that way sometimes, especially if the birth is

129

difficult. Lucy was her father's little girl. They were mad about each other. Your mother was a bit shut out, I think. After the accident she talked about a fresh start, but it only meant what suited her. She never let your father forget what had happened, but she never let him talk about it either, not even to me. That was the beginning of his drinking. And of course she never let him near you. You were her pride and joy, and she'd snatch you up if he so much as bent over the cot. Making out she could never trust him again, you see.'

'I still don't understand what happened, Gran,' Mark said crossly.

'Don't you?' She looked at him in surprise. 'Oh, haven't I said yet? It was your dad's fault that Lucy fell in, you see. He was supposed to be minding her and he let her wander off towards the lake while he was watching the putting on the green.'

Mark's chest was suddenly so tight he could hardly get his breath. 'You mean it happened in the park?'

She nodded rapidly. It was her turn to be impatient. 'Isn't that just what I've been saying? She wandered off the path into the water. It was just by the boathouse, so you'd think someone would have stopped her. Two lads in a rowing boat fished her out. It was only by the edge, but it was a little pocket of deep water. She was wearing the red coat I bought her.'

They were both silent, each following the path of their own thoughts. At last Mark said hesitantly, not daring to look at her, 'Gran, what do you think happens to people when they die?'

She glared at him. 'What's that got to do with anything?'

Mark was utterly confused. 'Well, if Lucy could communicate, that would explain . . .' he began, and stopped. His grandmother was staring at him as if he was mad.

'I thought you knew,' she said. 'Lucy isn't dead. They got her heart started again, but there was a lot of brain damage. She's in a home near your auntie's. Your mother goes to see her once a month.'

CHAPTER TEN

When Mark left, his grandmother went down with him to the main entrance. It was supper time and other residents were progressing slowly towards the dining hall, where the smell of food had intensified. As they reached the door, his grandmother laid her hand on his arm.

'So you promise you won't tell them who told you?'

Mark rolled his eyes. 'Gran, I've already said it about a million times. I won't get you into any trouble with Mum.' He hoped he wouldn't, anyway.

'Here.' She fumbled with the catch of her handbag, which hung in the crook of her bad arm. 'Let me give you something to buy yourself a few sweets.'

'*Gran*—' He looked around, embarrassed, but nobody was paying any heed.

'Now don't try and tell me you don't like them,' she said. 'Last time you brought me some chocolates, you ate most of them yourself.'

'Those weren't my chocolates, they were Mum's,' Mark said.

'Well, whoever's they were, I didn't see many of them,' she retorted. 'Now, let's see if I can find...' She took out her purse and made him hold it while she peered into it, poking at this coin and that. Mark couldn't help noticing several pound coins, and he wondered if he should point them out. Finally she extracted something and pressed it into his hand.

'Get yourself some mints,' she said. 'They're nice, mints are.'

Mark stared down at the twenty pence coin in disbelief. 'Thanks, Gran,' he said. 'I'll try not to spend it all at once.'

'I don't mind how you spend it,' she said. 'Take care of yourself, now.' She touched his hand and set off for the dining hall. Mark pocketed the money with a grin and went out into the street.

It was dark and cold now. With his head down and his hands plunged in his pockets, Mark began to walk away from the direction of the home. It was tea time and the road through the estate was quiet except for a group of boys on bikes riding up and down without lights. Noises reached Mark occasionally from the houses he passed; raised voices, a door slamming, the yammering signature tune of the news. Through the gaps in living room curtains he had glimpses of families, small children in pyjamas running about, and older ones eating with their parents in front of the television. It gave him a strange feeling to be outside, as if he would never be indoors in the warm again. After a while he stopped looking in at the windows and just walked with his eyes on the pavement ahead of him until his legs felt shaky with tiredness.

Without really noticing where he was going, he had come out quite close to where Tim lived. He recognised the Methodist church and the little row of shops. He wasn't sure if he wanted to see Tim, but habit and loneliness took him as far as the top of Tim's street. This was a row of large, rather run-down terraced houses, some of them divided into bedsits or flats. Tim's house was about halfway down. When Mark reached it, he saw a light behind the sagging curtains of the living room and another in Tim's room at the top of the house, but it was another minute before he brought himself to open the gate and walk down the path to the door. For all he knew, Craig could be there.

To his surprise, almost to his relief, no one answered the bell. He rang again, moving away down the path in expectation of no reply. But this time there was a response. He heard movement just behind the door, the flap of the letterbox trembled and Tim's voice, shrill and fearful, came out of it: 'If that's you, Craig, you can just piss off. I've put the chain on, *and* the back door's locked.'

Mark went right up to the door. 'It's me,' he said. 'It's Mark. Open up.'

'*Who?* I can't hear you.'

Mark bent down and put his mouth to the letterbox. '*Mark*,' he bellowed. 'Let me in, will you?'

There was a pause, then Tim said again, 'Who?' He sounded querulous, almost tearful. Any moment now, Mark realised, he would just give up and go back to his room. Quickly he felt in his pocket, found a library ticket and dropped it through the slit. After a long moment he heard the scrabble of the chain being undone, and the door swung open.

Tim had been crying. He looked about ten years old with the dirty tear marks on his face. Mark followed him into the living room, where ethnic rugs hid the holes in the carpet. The ashtray on the coffee table had been made by Tim's mum at evening classes, as had the funny metal sculpture on the mantelpiece. One of the family's dogs, an elderly black labrador, lay basking along the length of the radiator. Tim squatted down beside it and squeezed it passionately round the neck.

'I should have set Gripper on them, shouldn't I, Gripper?' Despite being half-throttled, the dog responded only with a faint thump of its tail on the carpet.

'He's hardly a Rottweiler, though, is he?' Mark felt obliged to point out. 'I don't exactly see Craig shaking in his shoes at the thought of Gripper being set on him. He looks as if he's forgotten how to bark, let alone how to bite.'

He knew he'd overdone it even before he finished speaking. Tim tightened his hold on Gripper's neck and said, almost hysterically, 'He's my *friend*. Aren't you, Gripper? You'd have sent them packing, wouldn't you, boy?'

Mark decided to wait before he spoke again. For a minute or two the only sound was the asthmatic wheeze of Gripper's breathing as Tim patted and stroked his head.

'So what have they been doing to you, anyway?' Mark asked as soon as he thought it safe. 'I thought you and Craig were such great mates.' The note of triumph crept into his voice however hard he tried to prevent it.

Tim reddened. 'I don't know if I want to tell you.'

'Please yourself,' Mark said, offended. 'I won't tell you what's happened to me, either.' He hadn't realised, until he spoke, that he wanted to, that his walk had been no accident after all.

Tim looked at him with faint curiosity. 'What has happened, then?'

'No, you first,' Mark insisted. His was

too difficult. And if Tim's story made him look small, then that was his own fault for going off with Craig in the first place.

'We'll have to go upstairs, then,' Tim said. He got to his feet, looking wretched.

'Up to your room, do you mean?' Mark said.

Tim nodded, and led the way to the door. He didn't speak as they climbed the stairs, but when they reached the top landing he hurried forward and stood in front of the door with his back to it, blocking the way. His expression was odd, he looked white and excited, as if he was about to be sick.

'Mark,' he said, 'if I let you in, you've got to promise not to tell, especially not anyone at school. Understand?'

'Sure,' Mark said, surprised. 'Whatever you say.'

Tim moved aside, and Mark had to open the door himself.

Inside the room, Tim's models were scattered everywhere, or parts of them were. Some had been stamped on and the pieces ground into the carpet or hurled across the room. Others lay smashed at the foot of the walls. Scissors and a hammer lay on the floor near the bed. Even the posters and magazines had been ripped up and scattered in shreds across the room. Mark looked back at Tim in horror.

'Did Craig—? Oh, Jesus.' He stepped forward. Under his feet, pieces of plastic crackled and broke. He stooped and picked up a bit of wing with the transfers still on it, and looked round foolishly for other parts of the same plane.

'*Don't*,' said Tim in a voice full of anguish. 'Don't, don't. Just leave it alone, Mark.'

Mark dropped it as if it was burning. Tim stepped over the threshold carefully and stood on a piece of clearer ground.

'Next week,' Mark said unevenly, 'next Saturday, Tim, we'll go the model shop and I'll buy you some more. I've got some money saved.'

But Tim shook his head. 'I want the ones I had,' he said. 'I don't want new ones.' He sat down on the edge of the bed and picked up the scissors. He began to play with them, opening and shutting them and running his thumb along the blade.

It hardly mattered really, but Mark asked, 'So how did it happen, I mean, what started them off?'

'Oh, it's a bit complicated,' Tim said. 'That's part of why I don't want you to tell.' The scissors screamed faintly as he opened and shut them. 'I think Craig only kept coming round here because of Kate.'

'Kate?' Mark was startled. Kate was Tim's sister, next up from him, which would make her about sixteen. She was a hunt saboteur and a campaigner for animal rights. She wore long Indian skirts and a nose stud and dyed her short hair with henna. At school she belonged to a group of girls who called themselves feminist anarchists and were always getting into trouble for writing graffiti in the toilets. She despised Tim. Mark couldn't imagine her liking any boy, let alone a boy like Craig.

'The first time he came round, she was really rude to him,' Tim said. 'Well, you know what she's like. But Craig thought that was great. Next time he came, he left

140

me and Graham watching telly and went up to see her in her room. He often did it after that. Graham used to go and listen at the door, and he said they were—you know, at it. But I couldn't tell what they were doing. All you heard through the door was laughing and talking. I asked Kate once and she told me to piss off. Anyway, when Craig was with Kate, Graham used to get really fed up with me on his own. He used to mess about with my planes and try and wind me up, you know, opening the windows and pretending he was going to drop them out and stuff. Then tonight he started chucking them around.' Tim swallowed hard. 'I ignored him to start with, but that only made it worse. First he started chucking them onto the floor and against the wall. I shouted at him to stop and the others must have heard, because they came up. I was hanging onto Graham's back by this time, pulling at his arms to try and make him stop. Craig didn't know what to do when he saw us. He started to laugh, but he was looking at Kate all the time to see what she thought. She said, "Chuck us one,

Graham," and then they were all at it, throwing them backwards and forwards, with me running about in between. And then Kate yelled, "Let's finish them off properly. Destroy all war machines!" And she went downstairs and came back with the hammer and scissors.'

Mark was scandalised. 'Aren't you going to tell your mum?'

Tim twisted the scissors round his finger. 'She doesn't like me saying things against the girls. She says I have to stick up for myself.'

'Then tell her about Kate and Craig,' Mark said, viciously.

'Oh, she wouldn't mind about that,' Tim said, surprised. 'If they really are doing anything, I mean. She says it's up to the girls to say yes or no for themselves. My dad has a fit about it when he comes round. But Mum says she isn't a policeman.'

Mark's opinion must have shown in his face, for Tim lifted up his chin defensively. 'Mum says, why should she be a hypocrite? She does what she wants, so why shouldn't we?'

Mark decided to say nothing. The

faint screaming of the scissors resumed. Then Tim said, 'I hate this house. Next time my dad comes, I'm going to ask if I can live with him.'

CHAPTER ELEVEN

In the end Mark left without telling Tim about Lucy. Tim seemed to have forgotten there was anything to tell, and once they came downstairs again and Mark saw the time, he was filled with alarm about what might be happening at home. Things only got worse by being put off, he thought uneasily. He should have gone straight back after seeing Gran. But when he stood outside the house and saw the light shining through the thin blue curtains of the living room into the street, he felt differently. They were inside, waiting for him.

He slid his key into the lock, acutely aware of the slight noise it made as he turned it and opened the door. It closed behind him with a thud and he stood in the hall and listened. They must have known he was there, they must have heard him, but there was no sound of any response. He had a brief vivid image of them on the other side of the wall, rigid and listening. His hand moved towards the handle of the living room door, but as he pushed it open he stood to one side so as not to be seen. He saw floral carpet, his mother's empty chair, the rug in front of the gas fire, then his father's grey trousers and slippered feet. Mark stepped forward into his line of view. For a few moments his father said nothing. His face was blotched red and white and his hand, holding a glass, trembled slightly.

'I thought it was your mother,' he said. 'She's gone out looking for you. If she couldn't find you, she was going to start ringing the hospitals.' The note of fear in his voice unnerved Mark.

'I was only walking round town,' he said. 'I went to see Gran. I didn't mean you to worry.' But he did. He did. He realised that he did.

'I thought I'd lost you.' His father sounded dazed. 'I thought you'd gone out and done something stupid, got

144

yourself run over.' There was no hostility in his voice, no accusation, just shock and love.

'I didn't mean it,' Mark stammered out, coming nearer. He was at sea; the landmarks were flooded out. 'I'm sorry,' he cried. 'I was upset, I didn't think—'

'It's all right.' His father rubbed his knees. 'It's all right. You're here now. That's all that matters.'

They stared at each other again like startled animals.

'So you went to see your gran?' his father resumed. 'I didn't even think of that. Your mother phoned someone from the school and they said you hadn't been in all day. Then she tried that friend of yours—Tim, is it?—and got no answer.'

Mark began to puzzle over times. 'I did go there,' he said. 'It must have been just before, when there was all the trouble.'

'You went to his place, then? Your mother thought you might. All I could think of was—was accidents. Because of you being upset. I'm sorry I went off like that earlier, Mark, but I couldn't help it.

I was that upset, I just had to get out, get away. I had a few drinks, then I went to the library and tried to think. Things have never been easy between us, I know that. All your life, it seems like I've been watching you at a distance. I never could get close. Sometimes when I've had a bit too much of this,' he swirled the whisky in his glass, 'I've tried to show you how I feel. But you always looked as if you despised me and I thought, fair enough. There's a lot to despise. And you're clever, and you've got your mother, so I thought, fair enough. He doesn't need me. Better off without.'

It was almost too painful for Mark to bear. He started to say something, anything, but his father held up a hand.

'Don't interrupt me, Mark, or I'll never get through it. I'm not very good with words, as you know. When you said what you said earlier, I got very scared. I thought, if he finds out about that, it'll be the end. He'll really hate me. But the more I thought about it, the more it seemed as if you had a right to be told. You seemed so desperate to know, so upset that I made up my mind to tell you.

I came home about four, expecting that you'd be in shortly. I waited and I waited and I began to think of all the things that might have happened to you and I couldn't have borne it. Not after last time. Not again.'

'Dad.' Mark's eyes were full of tears. 'Dad, it's all right.'

'But you don't *know*,' he said.

'Yes, I do,' said Mark. 'Gran told me.'

'All of it?'

Mark nodded. His father took a long swallow of whisky and water. 'That's that then,' he said. 'You know what to think of me.'

'I know what to think,' Mark said unsteadily. He reached down and wrung his father's hand. 'That's why you watched the girls at my school, isn't it?' he said. 'At one point I really thought—' he trailed off, regretting it.

But his father didn't seem to have noticed. 'I think about her all the time,' he said softly. 'All the time. What she would have been like. When I see a young girl that looks a bit like her, a little one, or a teenager, or one of these students now. She'd have made a good

147

student. She was a clever little thing.'

Mark felt a curious pang. 'But you never go and see her,' he said.

His father's eyes slid away. 'Your mother goes,' he said. 'She keeps in touch. Not that Lucy notices. I went once, Mark. I couldn't after that.'

Mark said nothing. He felt—he didn't know what he felt. Jealousy, perhaps.

They might have moved anyway, but when the front door banged, they sprang apart.

'He's back,' Mark's father called, sounding nervous.

The living room door opened. She stood in the doorway, her tights and blunt-toed navy shoes spattered with muddy water. Mark lifted his eyes to her face. It was chalk white; she looked ill with anger.

'Sorry, Mum,' he whispered.

To his infinite distress she ignored him. In silence she unbuttoned her coat and flung it down on the floor between the settee and the chair, then bent down to take off her shoes. As she did so, Mark stepped forward to pick up her coat.

'Leave that alone,' she snarled.

'I was only—'

'I told you, leave it alone!' Her eyes met his with rage. 'Do you think I want you to touch anything of mine after what you did to me today?'

'What do you mean?' Mark said in a panic. 'What have I done? I haven't done anything.'

She couldn't, or wouldn't, reply. She put one hand on the arm of the settee for balance and began to peel off her wet tights. Then she straightened up, clutching them in her fist, and looked at him.

'You know what you've done,' she said, her voice unnaturally high and shaky. 'You know what you've done, Mark Robson. You've tried to undermine everything I've worked for, everything I've struggled to get. And you've succeeded, so I hope you're happy. I hope you're happy, Mark, because I'm—' Her voice cracked and she stopped talking and started to cry.

'Don't, Mum, please don't,' Mark said, distressed. He moved towards her, but again she warded him off.

'If you think those lads at school bully

you now, how do you think they'll be once they know about *her*?' she sobbed. 'You tell me that. How do you think I'll feel going in to work, when it's all been stirred up again, and everyone's looking at me, pitying me, and asking questions? It was bad enough when it happened, bad enough having everyone talking, whispering about us, *pitying* us. They'd all forgotten, but you'll start it all up again, won't you? You won't be able to keep your mouth shut. You'll make us all *abnormal*.' She glared at him, wiping her eyes on her sleeve. 'And the worst of it is, you blame me. No, just you shut up and let me speak. You blame me for lying and covering up, and wanting things nice. Well, I do want things nice. There's nothing wrong in that, is there? I wanted things nice for *you*. I wanted us to be a normal happy family. I thought if I brought you up not knowing, you'd be able to love and respect your dad, even if *I* knew—' Her voice rose uncontrollably and she had to stop. Her hands kneaded the tights for a moment and then she shouted, almost screamed, 'I'm the one that's held this family together when it was falling apart. I'm the one that goes to see her, for Christ's sake!'

The silence that followed was filled with her quiet, hopeless sobbing. Mark's father sat rigid, staring at the wall. Mark was afraid to speak. He was afraid to approach her. She was so hurt. At last he said brokenly, 'I'm glad I know.'

She lifted her head.

'I'm glad I know, Mum,' he repeated. 'I thought I was going mad.'

She didn't ask what he meant. With a shuddering sigh, she seemed to pull herself together. 'I suppose it was your gran that told you,' she said, feeling in her sleeve for a tissue. 'I presume that's where you were this evening.'

'No, I was at Tim's,' Mark said uneasily.

'I see,' said his mother. 'Telling him all about it. But it was your gran that told you, wasn't it? I'll have something to say to her next time I'm at that home.'

'It wasn't Gran,' Mark said, alarmed. He had promised to keep her out of it. 'It wasn't her. I can't tell you who it was. I promised not to.'

His mother flushed a dark angry red.

151

'You'll tell me, all right. You'll tell me if we have to stay up all night to get it out of you.'

Mark lowered his head, saying nothing.

'I'm waiting,' his mother said in a brittle, dangerous voice. 'I want to know who I have to thank for all this.'

Mark's father stirred in his chair. 'Jean—' he said uneasily.

'You stay out of it,' she snapped. 'Mark, you're not leaving the room until you've told me. I mean that.'

Mark knew she did. He could feel the terrible pressure of her expectation, and he wanted, idiotically, to laugh. He knew it would be a disaster if he did. Almost without meaning to, he blurted it out.

'It was Lucy. She told me herself. I thought she was a ghost, but she isn't, she's alive. It must have been, what do you call it, telepathy.' He forgot to worry about what she thought. He was filled with an extraordinary relief. His life was on the map again. Telepathy, that was what they called it. Claire would know, of course.

His mother reached out and slapped

his face. He was astonished more than hurt. She had never hit him in his life that he could remember. She, too, seemed shocked at herself. As Mark gingerly touched his burning cheek, she stared at him, breathing quickly.

'How dare you? How *dare* you say a thing like that. After the hours I've spent at her bedside, waiting and waiting, and then to have you try and pretend that your attention grabbing tricks are more than—oh, you make me sick.'

Behind him, Mark heard his father stand up. 'I think that's enough now, Jean,' he said.

She turned on him, smiling bitterly. 'It's a bit late in the day for you to get involved, isn't it?'

'Very,' he agreed. 'All the same, I think you should let it go.'

'Let it go?' she echoed, outraged. 'Let it go? That's been the story of your life so far, hasn't it? Let everything go, and just sit, with your ears and eyes closed, while others struggle on without you. Well, I'm sorry, but I'm not letting this go. I want to know who told him. All those stupid tricks, writing her name

153

everywhere, carrying on like he was mad. I want to know who put him up to it.'

'What's it matter, since it wasn't us?' Mark's father said. 'What's it matter who told him? We didn't, and we should have, Jean. We should have. You know we should.'

She looked at him and her mouth started to tremble. 'I've had to do everything on my own,' she said. 'On my own, Alan.'

Awkwardly, Mark's father put a hand on her shoulder and caressed her. 'I know, love,' he said. 'I'm sorry.'

She closed her eyes. When she opened them again, she looked at Mark.

'Perhaps we should have told you,' she said. 'I don't know. I shouldn't have hit you, anyway. I just got beyond myself. It wasn't right, that.' She smiled, or tried to, and held out her hand. Mark took it gladly, and tried to smile back. He hoped everything would be all right now. But the only one of them who seemed sure about anything was his dad.

'Why don't you go up to bed now, love?' he said. 'You've got an early start tomorrow. You don't want one of your heads coming on.'

She nodded. 'I think I will,' she said quietly. 'Don't be too long coming upstairs, Mark. You've got school tomorrow.'

As soon as the door was safely shut, Mark said, 'Will she be all right?'

His father smiled. 'I think so. I've been a fool, Mark. I should have had it all out with her years ago. I was just taking the easy way out, letting her have it her own way. It was easier for me, but it wasn't good for any of us.' He sat down and poured himself a large whisky.

There was still one thing Mark felt he had to get straight. 'It was true what I said,' he muttered. 'It was Lucy who told me. Gran only explained the details.'

'What?' It was obvious his father wasn't listening. 'Mark, you like history, don't you?'

It was such a *non sequitur* Mark was baffled. 'Yes, I do. Why?'

'I was thinking we could go over to Castleton on Saturday and look round the industrial museum. I feel like an outing.'

He had never made an offer like that

before. It filled Mark with a mixture of pleasure and alarm.

'I'd like to,' he said cautiously. 'Only I promised Tim I'd go into town with him.'

'Bring him as well, then,' said his father.

Mark thought it over. 'I suppose I could,' he conceded. 'He should be at school tomorrow.' Both school and tomorrow seemed infinitely remote. He yawned hugely and tiredness hit him like a drug. 'Sorry, Dad,' he said. 'I think I'd better go to bed.'

His father seemed faintly disappointed. 'All right, if you have to,' he said. 'But I think I'll finish this one before I go up.' He took a big swallow, then looked at Mark and laughed self-consciously. 'It won't be long before you'll be dragging me into pubs, will it, son?' he said.

Mark hesitated. 'I don't actually like whisky very much,' he said.

His father cleared his throat, a bit embarrassed. 'Oh, well then. We'll have to find something else to do together. That's all I meant.'

'I'd like that,' Mark said. ''Night, then.'

''Night,' said his father. 'See you in the morning.'

Mark went upstairs, undressed and lay down. He was too exhausted to sleep or think. As soon as he closed his eyes his head was filled with a noisy and chaotic film: Tim, Win, Gran, Mr Potter, all had their idiotic say and moved at impossible speed in and out of view. Shut up, shut up, shut up: I am so tired. But he could not switch them off. Finally he sat up, opened his eyes and stared wearily at the hillocks of his knees. Gradually he drifted into a grey daze that got blacker and blacker until the light at the window and the noises downstairs woke him again and it was day. He was lying with the covers half over his face and his thumb in the corner of his mouth. He wondered if Lucy would ever contact him again.

CHAPTER TWELVE

The school hall was almost full. Mark sat on stage with other members of the wind band, craning his neck round the tall clarinettist in front of him to see the audience. It was stupid to try, really, only everyone else was doing it, spotting parents and sisters or brothers, giving them a grin or a wave. From where he was sitting he couldn't even see the door, and the piano cut off his view of most of the hall. He told himself his parents were probably there, but he couldn't help going on looking. He wouldn't really believe they had both come until he saw them.

In the ten minutes that the band had been waiting on stage, occasional whispering had grown into an excited buzz. The third year trombonists behind Mark were pinching each other and sniggering. Below them, in the string section, someone—Mark hoped it wasn't Claire—made a wild adjustment to a music stand, which promptly collapsed, scattering sheets of music all over the place. Mr Potter, struggling in the wings to tune the violin of a nervous first year soloist, swore audibly.

'One of you pick up the music. Not you, Susie! And if you lot don't all settle down and shut up, I'll take you off the stage and start with the girls' choir! And yes, I do mean it, Derek, so you can take that silly grin off your face.'

Feeling guilty, Mark sat back in his chair, balanced his immaculately polished trumpet on his knees, and folded his arms to wait. But it was hard not to feel silly, strange and excited when the air was full of the smell of soap and fresh ironing, and everyone's hair was combed and their instruments gleaming and there were only minutes to go before Mr Moynihan got up on the platform to make his speech. Mark went through the order of pieces in his mind. Five German dances and the Purcell for the full orchestra; then a string solo, a woodwind trio, and finally his own. Claire wouldn't play her solo until after the interval, which was a relief as he had enough to be nervous about on his own account. Sweat prickled on his palms and the pleasant excitement lurched into anxiety. It would be all right, he tried to reassure himself; he went over the phrasing of the piece again and hummed a tricky bit. But playing badly was not the worst of it. His solo was the piece he had played out of the window for Lucy less than a month ago.

He looked back at it now as if through his fingers, trying to protect himself. I was crazy, he thought, amazed. I must have been mad. It needed only a glimpse to fill him with pain and shame. Not that he had done anything so very terrible, but the memory of his own feelings still left him horribly exposed. His parents, after that first evening, had not talked about what had happened, preferring to act as if he had known about Lucy all along. He understood why; it was easier for both of them, especially his mother, but it made it impossible for him to approach the question that really troubled him. Even with Claire he had avoided it, preferring to let her theorise alone. It was simply too painful to think about, having seen Lucy at last. What communication was possible, after all, with a life so hidden? It would have been simpler to credit all that had happened to the powers of his own mind, if he only could; to believe his subconscious had staged everything, out of memories and guesses.

Seeing Lucy had really shaken him. He had gone to the hospital two weeks ago, undertaking the exhausting journey with his mother, four hours each way and an hour at the hospital beside a giant pram. Lucy lay on her side, under white airtex blankets. He would have liked to reach out and touch her clenched fingers, wipe her slack mouth, but he was afraid. Only her hair was beautiful, a pale corn colour, short and very fine. Before coming he had hoped for a signal, a sign, no matter how faint, of recognition. But there was nothing. She banged her head rhythmically, and once or twice she made a noise, a high-pitched remote sound like nothing human, nothing known. Mark understood why his father could not bear it. His mother, sitting opposite, stared at her hands in her lap until the hour was up, then went for a word with the nurse. On the way home neither she nor Mark spoke. There was too much to talk about.

* * *

In the school hall, they were at last ready to begin. Everyone suddenly grew quiet as Mr Moynihan stepped up onto the stage and began his speech. It was funny to hear him praising the school in the same tired voice he used for issuing final warnings at morning assembly. Soon he handed over to Mr Potter, who gave a summary of the year's musical achievements. Mark was able to listen without jealousy. Yesterday his father had signed the form that would allow him to do GCSE music. He was glad, of course, very glad, but he felt uncomfortable about how he had managed it. He had brought out the form again on the last day possible, but this time he had asked his father to sign it. He knew from his mother's face what she thought, but she didn't actually say it. She didn't say many things outright any more. She had lost her old certainty, and Mark himself missed it.

His father had signed quite happily and then started to talk about his own time in a youth orchestra playing the clarinet. Apparently, that was how his parents met; his mother played the flute in the same band. Mark hadn't heard this story before; he didn't know his dad had ever played anything. So they went on talking about music through the rest of the evening's television, his mother putting in the odd word, but never directed towards him. Once or twice he caught her looking at him, but she immediately looked away. It made Mark feel like a traitor, but he took the form to school this morning anyway. This evening, when he came home, she had been in a terrible temper, flaring up about nothing and threatening not to come to the concert because she had a bad head. Both of them knew what she was really angry about, but neither of them came out with it. He hoped Dad had managed to persuade her to come after all.

*　　*　　*

Mr Potter had finished speaking and turned to face the band. Mark sat up, alert now, and ready with his trumpet at his lips, watching the baton. When it rose he came in a fraction early, the trombones were late, and the first bars were ragged and out of tune. Frowning tremendously, Mr Potter rose on his toes and sawed away with his arms, urging them all together. The second of the five short dances was better, and the third went with a swing. After that it was easy. The Purcell came out, measured and sweet, and Mark felt no compulsion to rush the top line or play too loudly, as he often did. The applause was enthusiastic and, as he sat back and met the grins and glances of the players round him, Mark wished they could all go on playing in full ensemble, with no nerve-racking solos, play on until the interval and then disappear safely home.

The first soloist, the violinist, crept out from the second desk and wriggled past the music stands to the front of the stage. Mr Potter sat down at the piano and, when she nodded, began to play the accompaniment. She began timidly and was gaining confidence when, halfway through the piece, she broke down, looking across at Mr Potter with agony in her eyes. She was a thin dark girl, flat-chested and frail looking. As Mr Potter spoke to her encouragingly, Mark could see her hands were trembling. She began again and got past the difficulty, only to break down in another place. The trombonists behind Mark guffawed openly. The girl returned to her seat in tears, to sympathetic and embarrassed applause. Mark looked down, feeling heat in his own face, anticipating his own disaster.

The woodwind trio assembled hastily and launched into the theme from the Surprise Symphony by Haydn. As Mark watched the clarinettist, his thoughts returned to his father. Dad said he was looking for a job. He read all the adverts in the evening paper and cut out the ones he liked, but so far they'd never got further than a yellowing heap on the floor beside his chair. Mum tried to throw them out when she tidied up, but Dad gave her such an argument that usually she just left them. Maybe something would come of them one day. Maybe.

The trio swung into 'Home on the Range'. Mark fiddled with his trumpet mouthpiece and sat forward in his seat. Any minute now—and they had finished. As the applause broke, he made his way forward, skirting round the edge of the stage to the front. His heart was thumping and his hands were clammy. The audience were very close, the first upturned faces only a few feet away. He peered out, fighting fear like vertigo, thinking, please God, let them have come, please God, both of them: and then he saw them, two or three rows back behind the piano, sitting together, staring up at him with anxious faces. He glanced across at Mr Potter, raised his trumpet and began. His first notes were strained and hesitant. There was a pit in his stomach because they were both there and he was frightened of making a mistake. He had to play for all of them, for his parents, for Lucy, for himself; for the compromise and the confusion, the little patch of darkness inside them all.

But the music came out of that. There wasn't anywhere else it could come from. With the knowledge, he was suddenly lifted. His fingers slipped into obedience; he knew, with exultation, how it must be played. And as he finished, he looked at their faces. His father was applauding frantically, but his mother sat very still with her hands in her lap. Hurt flared up, then subsided as Mark took in the expression on her face. She was still listening. She had heard him.

Mr Potter stood up, grinning and mouthing something, and briefly joined in the applause. 'Excellent! *Excellent!*' Something like that. But Mark waited until they had all finished.

'That was for my sister,' he said into their silence, and walked back to his place in the band.